Damaged Daddy Next Door

A Friends to Lovers Single Dad Romance

Emma Lena

Contents

Chapter 1

MICHAEL

One year ago. Saturday. 9:15 p.m.

Saturday is my only free day, and while I would have preferred to spend it all with Laura, she insists on not seeing another living soul until noon.

I am a doctor, an orthopedic surgeon, so my hours are not that flexible either. I am also an investor, though that does not take as much of my time in a day as a doctor's hours do. I mostly invest through my bankers and lawyers. But, I go through the details of whatever company or property I am looking to invest in, myself.

I have always been interested in the business world, but my passion to heal surpassed wheeling deals. It is a passion on its own and I love it even more because I realize I am really good at it. A good chunk of my money comes from my investments. Over the past year, I have made millions in investing, and when Levy had calculated my net worth at the end of last year, he had informed me I was now a billionaire.

Even though I had not really been surprised at how much I made investing, I was still a little surprised I had made it into the billionaire region. But, I guess when you add my profits from my investments and my salary from my job, to my inheritance which I had barely touched ever since it had been released in college.... yeah, I could see being a billionaire. I don't keep tabs on things like that. I am not dense about my finances, but I mostly leave the big chunks of it to Levy, as I completely trust him.

My fiancé, Laura is an artist and an illustrator. She works part-time for a children's books company, *Innocence*. In her free time, which is usually somewhere from 9:00 a.m. to 12:00 p.m., she works on a personal project of hers. She is creating a manga series, and I don't know much about it because she doesn't like to talk about it while it's not yet finished. I respect her need for aloneness as a part of her creative process. Thus, I'm usually at her place by 12:05. She usually has illustrations to submit to *Innocence*, and some past work to brush up on. But, by mid-afternoon, she's done with work, and we usually have the rest of the day to ourselves. That is my favorite part of her schedule.

But before I can be with her, I waste away the hours with Levy, my best friend, over at his house. He had asked me how everything was going with Laura, and I had told him things were good.

He had given me a look and flipped the hotdog he was grilling, before saying, "I'm surprised, honestly. She doesn't seem like the type that stick around for long."

I had laughed away Levy's comment and said something like "What? It's not like she wears a sign on her back or something?"

I wrap my hands around Laura now and bring her even closer to my body. Her back is to my chest, we are both naked under the covers. The orange light from the bedside lamp spills over her face, highlighting her mesmerizing features. I close my eyes with a sigh as I smell her hair. She always smells of jasmine. Whether she has on the jasmine-scented perfume that I bought for her on her birthday, or not, she always smells like jasmine. Her honey-brown hair spills over my chest in waves of curls. I trace the tiny cleft in her chin with my hand, loving the way her lips curl up in a lazy smile. And right at this moment, she doesn't look like someone who wanted to be anywhere else but here with me.

Her eyes are closed, but I know behind the closed lids, her eyes are bluer than the color blue itself. I have gotten lost in those eyes more than a few times.

"So, how was work today?" I ask. My tone is lazy, I am so relaxed that any more relaxed, I think I'd be dead.

Her eyes are still closed, and Laura shrugs my question. "It was fine. Same as always."

I trail a finger behind her ear. My heart skips at her little shiver. I put my lips to her ear. "You going to let me read your manga series?" I whisper in her ear.

Laura sighs, snuggling even more against me. Her eyes are still closed. "Nope," she says plainly.

I drop flight kisses from the back of her ear down to her neck. "Come on. Let me read. Come on," I cajole her, still trailing kisses around her neck. I bite her a little and she giggles.

I get on top of her, my body not quite touching hers. I lift myself up on both my arms.

"Open your eyes," I whisper. I watch as she slowly opens her eyes, giving me the full effect of those raven-blue eyes. I smile down at her. "Let me read your book," I say again.

The lazy satisfaction in Laura's eyes gets replaced by mild annoyance. She sighs.

"We've been over this, Michael. I told you, I don't like anyone reading my stuff till it's done."

"I know. But make an exception for me. Hmm?" I kiss her on her forehead, her nose, and then her lips. "For me," I say before finally removing my lips from hers.

We kiss for the next minute, and then let up for air. I look down at her, into her eyes, sure of my victory.

She smirks at me. "No."

I groan and drop my forehead against hers. She laughs. She lifts my head from her forehead and runs her fingers through my hair.

"I don't crack that easy, mister."

She kisses me on the lips and then pushes me back on the bed. She jumps up off the bed and walks naked to the mirror on the reading table in the room.

I let my head drop on the pillow, and look up at the ceiling for a second. Then, I lift my head and let my eyes follow her movement. Laura has the perfect figure that I imagine most women wanted, and I know for a fact men salivate after. But her perfect figure hadn't been what attracted me to her when we first talked.

At our first encounter, Laura had been wearing an oversized sweater over baggy jeans. Her hair had not been brushed, seeing as it was an early morning, and we had met in a coffee shop. I had taken my first step into falling for her when she had turned, and those blue eyes had focused on me. Then, I had fallen like crazy when she gave me a rude 'What you looking at?' - look.

Two years later, and even though we just had the most mind-blowing sex we've ever had, the eyes are still the thing that gets me.

I cross my arms behind my head as I continue looking at my fill. My lips curve slightly. "Hey, what if we just made a baby?"

Slowly, Laura turns around to look at me. Her eyebrows furrow in a frown. She crosses her arms. "Why would you say something like that?" she asks.

I notice her clipped tone and defensive posture. "Hey, I was just joking," trying to dig myself out of the massive hole I just made for myself.

She grabs her robe from the edge of the bed, and puts it on, covering her creamy-white skin. She belts the robe with a few jerky movements.

"Well, it wasn't very funny," she says. She leaves the room.

I frown, baffled as to why the thought of a baby pisses her off so much.

Present day. Saturday. 10:25 a.m.

I push Julia's stroller as I walk down the street. People walk past us in comfortable summer clothes, some in sunglasses, and most with one beach drink in their hands. I look down at the Island Guide in my hand. It had been given to me by my agent, a conservative blonde with a stylish suit that had seem out of place in the relaxed atmosphere of Catalina Island, and a no-nonsense tone. She had given it to me after she had handed me the keys to the house I had rented for the six month vacation I planned to have. Just me and my best girl.

The guide tells me the street I'm on is called Crescent Avenue. Or, if I wanted to sound more like the locals, Front Street. Whatever it was called, the street was beautiful. We come upon a brightly tiled fountain. I pause a moment to admire the arrangement of the different floral-designed tiles. The weather is sub-tropical, with a little warmth tossed in. A gentle wind blows, I look down to check in on Julia in her stroller. Her eyes are open and on me, staring wide-eyed as she looks up. She was the only reason I had gotten up in the mornings for the month following Laura leaving me at the altar.

I look around the brightly lit house. The agent just left after handing the house keys to me. The house came fully furnished, seeing as I am only renting it for the next six months. I only rented a house because of Julia. If it had been only me, I would have probably just stayed in a hotel room.

Last week, Levy had finally been able to convince me to go on a vacation. "To get out of the house, and away from the memories," as he had put it. While I had seen reason in his thinking, I hadn't been able to take the step till last week.

Memories of Laura were still something.

But, again, I realized I had to move on because of Julia. After searching for a runaway bride for close to three months, and coming up with nothing, you start to get the hint. That maybe, just maybe, the person didn't want to be found.

My heart constricts painfully, as it always does anytime I think of Laura. If I wasn't a doctor, I would be worried about the amount of times it does that.

We pass shops displaying Island apparels and hand-crafted works, an ice-cream shop, a candy shop, and a boutique. My stomach growls, indicating my hunger. I look down at the guide book in my hand again. I peruse through the options, landing on Antonio's Pizzeria & Cabaret. I'm in the mood for something Italian.

I calculate the distance of the restaurant from where I and Julia are at currently, and I judge its' not far.

"Let's go have us some Antonio's," I say to Julia. She just looks at me, blinking her wide eyes. I laugh, and push her stroller to continue our walk.

Minutes later, we walk into the restaurant. The place isn't crowded, nor is it scanty, as most of the tables were filled up with people having one delicacy or the other. The restaurant is an open restaurant with long wooden chairs and an unobstructed view of the ocean. I take a seat at one of the chairs, setting Julia's stroller beside me. I look out at the view, and it's

breath-taking. The ocean lay wide open in front of me, blue and endless. I take a deep breath, my eyes closed.

We had stayed at the Pavilion hotel yesterday, when we had arrived at Catalina Island. It had been one of the best moments of my life. The hotel has a central courtyard with swaying palm trees in the middle and surrounding it. There was a cozy fire ring with chairs, where I had sat down and breathed in my first calming breath in months.

Sitting at that fire ring and smelling the ocean air, it had felt like I had finally stopped hurting for a bit, just for a bit. And that was all I had needed at that moment.

I look down at the only reason I get up in the mornings since Laura left me. Her eyes are open, and on me, staring wide-eyed as she looks up at me from her stroller. Julia. My miracle was the purest gift Laura ever gave me.

Even at just three months, her blue eyes cut through me. Her mother's eyes. I crouch to look into her eyes.

My heart is constricting painfully like there's not enough blood pumping in, and I just smile. I smile because I love this bundle of joy in a stroller. Ever since the day after, what was supposed to be mine and Laura's wedding day, I had opened my door in hopes that Laura was at the other end. Instead, I had found a baby swaddled in a blanket, in a basket, on my front porch. Julia had looked up at me, just like she was looking up at me right now, and I had felt my heart constrict with emotions.

"It's just you and me now, Doc," I say. 'Doc' is my nickname for Julia, as she saved me after Laura left. Now all I have to do is look at her, and I feel my heart swell with love.

Chapter 2

OLIVIA

Sunday. 10:00 a.m.

I drop my head on the check-out counter in my bakery, which was about to become a crime scene. The murder? Mine.

I raise my head slowly, and my mother's voice continues to drone on out of the cell phone I hold to my ear. I pull at my shoulder-length blonde hair, which is now sticking out at the sides due to my incessant pulling. I want to gouge my eyes out, but I'm unsure as to how to go about it. I would take bleeding out of my ears- anything that would stop this conversation I am currently having with my mother- but that would probably not be a pretty sight.

"I just want to know what was wrong with this one now. Seriously. What was wrong with Ethan?" she asks.

I roll my eyes because I know there is a God, and he has to save me from this torture.

My mother is currently asking me what it was I found wrong in my boyfriend, well, ex, now, that made me break up with him. And the answer to that question is... nothing. Absolutely nothing is wrong with Ethan. Ethan is a nice guy. Ethan is a successful real estate agent, with funny jokes and charming smiles. Ethan is freaking awesome.

But I can't very well tell my mother that. Because, to her, there has to be something wrong with him for me to break up with 'such a fine young man.'

And for once, I agree with her. This is why sometimes I find myself wondering why on earth I broke up with him. So, what if I didn't find him interesting anymore, and I started to dread his calls? Ethan was still the perfect partner. The problem was with me.

I rub a hand over my forehead, I can feel a headache brewing. It's a mild one, but still. Annoyance flickers through me. It's been two months since I broke things off with Ethan, and one would think my mother would have let it go by now, but of course, one would be wrong.

My mother's voice continues to drone on as she talks a mile a minute. I just let her voice fade into the background. From where I'm standing, behind the counter, I can see outside. The doors are glass, and I watch as people go on about their day. The weather is nice and summer-like, and people walk past my shop, *Heartfilled*, in pairs, groups, and singles.

Sometimes, I'm scared I won't find my person. Ethan is not the first boyfriend I broke up with for no apparent reason. Ever since high school, I have had the uncanny luck of dating only good guys. While other girls complained about bad boys who broke their hearts, I have never even felt what it was like to be heartbroken.

And it always comes to me at really weird moments, that maybe the one guy I finally commit to would be my bad guy. So, I don't commit.

The bell above the door chimes, and I look toward it. I heave a relieved sigh as I see a customer walk in.

"Okay, mom, a customer just walked in. I have to go now. Bye-bye." I cut the call on her stutters.

I look up as the customer and her two friends walk toward the counter. Marilyn Monroe. (Yeah, I'm on the fence only if that is her real name too.) She is a tall blonde with a model figure. Her blonde hair is long, straight, and treated, whereas mine is short, messy, and dull.

I don't compare myself to her, of course, But it's hard not to feel like a lazy slob next to Marilyn Monroe. The real one, and the one standing in front of me right now.

She smiles at me and leans in over the counter to give me our customary kiss-over-cheek air kisses. I tilt my left cheek, then my right cheek, and make kissing sounds. I smile back at her once we're done.

"Olivia," Marilyn says. She says my name like she's opening a present. Always.

"Marilyn," I say hers like I love what's in the present. Always.

Marilyn is nice enough, for a snob, and normally I wouldn't have taken her on as a client, but she carries the big bucks. Her father is loaded, and seeing as Marilyn is his only daughter and she is getting married to her 'gummy bear' a week from now, he is pulling out all the stops.

And, I need the big bucks. So, its' a perfect partnership.

Her perfect face crinkles slightly as she pouts. "I know you don't open today. So sorry for the inconvenience, babe."

Normally, I don't open shop on Sundays, but again, big bucks.

I wave her off. "It's no worries. I'm here to help you get the perfect cake for your perfect day."

There are a lot of things I don't normally do, that I'm doing for Marilyn. The biggest is that I don't normally take wedding clients. Marilyn would be my second bride-client. The first was my mother. Seven years ago. When she got remarried to Steve, her first love. It had been an overly-emotional situation, and even my cynical heart had melted at their story. And of course, my mother had made sure to lay on the mother-daughter card. Heavily.

I don't take wedding clients for the sole purpose of not wanting to be heavily involved in a ceremony that had to do with ever-afters and unverified promises. The best weddings, to me, are the ones where I just get to sit and enjoy the show, as a guest.

But, according to Marilyn, she had had my lemon meringue cupcake on a day she had been feeling exceptionally 'sucky.' A friend of hers had bought it for her, and my cupcakes had helped her feel 'a-okay'. (Her words). And so, she just had to have it for her reception desserts. Then she insisted that I had to bake her wedding cake and her entire reception menu- the baked portion.

I have to give it to Marilyn; She was one hell of a persuasive person.

And so, now, I'm here, on a Sunday, and attending to my most high-maintenance and the most cash flow client.

"Hey, I heard you and Ethan broke up. So sad." Marilyn takes my hand in her hers and looks at me with pity.

I look down at her manicured, and brightly pink painted nails which are covering my bare ones. I look back up at her. I found out just last week that Ethan and Rob 'Gummy bear' were close friends. I had hoped to keep that tiny but catastrophic news to myself, but apparently, she found out.

She gives me a look as if I had just told her my mother had cancer. "Ethan is such a catch though. Good-looking too. You must be devastated."

11

I pry my hand from hers. I give her my best polite smile. "I'm fine. Let's talk about your cake."

I look down at the cake book open on the counter. I can feel Marilyn's eyes on me still. I feel an odd tightening in my chest like there is not enough air for me to breathe. I frown, rubbing a hand over my chest. *What is happening to me? Why am I feeling this way?* I look up at Marilyn, and that damned pitiful stare is still on her face. I feel like the walls of the shop are closing in on me. I look around, confused.

I snap out of it as one of Marilyn's friend's voices trickles into my consciousness. "Catalina Island is a BFD. You are so lucky that's where Rob's taking you for your honeymoon," she says.

Marilyn sighs, and rolls her eyes, a smile on her face. "I know. He is such a sweetheart, my gummy bear."

The other friends chirp in. "I heard Taylor Swift has been there," she says, like she's revealing a secret in a high school cafeteria.

The first friend says, "Of course, she's been there. If I had the money to go to a place like this," she thrusts out her phone, showing pictures of Catalina Island on it, "I'll be there in a heartbeat."

I glance at her phone, and I see the overview of the island, and it's breath-taking. I see pictures of brightly lit houses with palm trees surrounding them. She clicks on one of the videos on the website, and a video of the beach on Catalina Island plays.

I feel the tensions around my chest loosening as I stare at the soothing video. Marilyn and her friends' voices fade into the background as I continue to stare at the video.

Later, Marilyn and her posse leave. As the door to the shop closes behind them, I take my phone and type 'Catalina Island' in the web search. As I scroll through, I smile, feeling better than I've felt in two months.

Chapter 3

MICHAEL

Tuesday. 9:15 a.m.

I slap the tin cans on the kitchen countertop. Once. Then I slap them together. Twice. I slap one of the tins on the countertop, then slap the other one on top of that one. I do this twice.

One day, during the first month after Laura left me, a documentary had been on, on TV. An African-life documentary. I hadn't even been watching because I was trying to calm down Julia; she had been crying. She has incidentally been crying for most of the whole month. And then a scene with some African kids- Nigerian, to be precise- came on, and they were playing with tin cans. Miraculously, Julia stopped crying. She wasn't sobbing or sniffing, she stopped crying entirely.

I held my breath, afraid to spoil the moment, and watched for a minute as she continued staring at the TV with somber blue eyes. I just simply closed my eyes as I savored the sweet sound of silence.

Ever since that day, I beat tin cans against each other to make my girl happy. Talk about weird parenting.

My phone rings. I tilt my hips to the side to bring out my phone from my sweatpants pocket. I answer the call as I see who's calling.

"Hey, man. What's up?"

"Hey. I'm good. How are you? How's the vacation coming? Get any sand in your legs yet?" Levy asks. It's his clever way of asking if I'd been to the beach.

"If I did, you'd feel it in your ears," I say.

Levy laughs. "Nice. It's nice to hear you joke again. That place must be good for you. How's my best girl?"

The jury is still out on whether Catalina is a good place for me, but, I look at Julia.

"She's good," smiling down at her.

"I bet she misses her Uncle Levy."

"Yeah, you're going to have to ask her that yourself. She cries less now, so, that's something," I say to Levy, still looking down at Julia in her stroller.

"That's nice. Hey, so, I have gotten started on the trust fund for her. The test results for the DNA you took before you left came back. It's positive. Like we had any doubts," Levy adds blatantly, and I can almost see him roll his eyes. "So, it's a go on all accounts."

I nod even though Levy can't see me. I had the DNA tests conducted because Levy said it would be needed to do any legal stuff I wanted to do and that would bind Julia and me together. Levy is my accountant.

We hadn't done it before Julia's birth as most people do, mainly because Laura had been stressed out about the pregnancy, and she just hadn't wanted to deal with any of it.

Because I know Levy can't see my nod, I say, "Okay. That's fine. Thanks again, man, for taking care of all of it."

Again, I can almost see Levy waving away my gratitude. "Hey, whatever, man. I love that girl like crazy, and you're my best friend. And I'm your accountant. You need more reasons why I'm the one who *should* be handling all this stuff?"

I grin. "Nah, I think that about covers it."

"You make it easy. Especially the money part. I mean, you have more than enough, meaning I don't have to look and squeeze out money from corners. Julia will be one comfortable child," Levy says.

"That's all I want. I want her to have the best possible life. You know, I figured I would donate some of it to charities when the time comes. But, now, while I will still donate, at least I now have a reason for the other half."

"Yeah, and she's a damn good reason too. All through high school to the end of college, Julia would be just fine. And then, when she's done, she's got a sizeable amount to start up whatever she wants to do." Levy says.

All these make me happy, really. Never really thought about being a billionaire until Levy told me I was one at the end of the year, last year. When he did, I never really thought about it even then. But now, I'm sure damn happy about it.

"Well, I hope she decides to be a doctor like her daddy."

"That why you call her Doc?" Levy asks.

"Among other reasons" thinking of the days after Laura left.

Levy snickers. "Well, good luck with that, my friend. Something tells me that little girl has got a really strong mind of her own. She'll do whatever she damn well please."

I smile. "I'm counting on it."

There is silence, then Levy says, "But, for real though, man, I think that place would be really good for you and Jules. As much as memories are very important- to keep important people in our minds and hearts, they are not very good when they are memories that hurt. Sometimes, moving on is the strongest thing we can ever do."

At random times like these, Levy, who mostly jokes around, says something deeply profound. When this happens, I'm almost convinced he's not the same person.

Then in a lighter tone, he says, "Let go, my friend. Get your beach shorts on. Your shades off, so you can see those beautiful tan ladies. Get sand on your feet, and water in your eyes. Keep Julia away from those teenage boys who think they are now men. I would hate to break someone's legs. And finally, do everything I would do."

And... he's back.

I shake my head. "On that last one? No, not a chance," and cut the call on Levy's laughter.

2:15 p.m.

I come out of my bedroom and walk through the living room, to answer the door. The doorbell rings again.

"I'm coming," I say under my breath.

I get to the door and open it. I see a man and a woman standing on my front steps. The man is about the same height as me, with black hair and eyes that sparkled like gems. He isn't laughing, just smiling, but his whole face seems to be happy about something. He is wearing a beach shirt over a white graphic tee, and beach shorts with palm sandals on his feet. The woman stands at a head shorter than him, and me. Her hair is a mixture of brown and blonde, and though her face is a happy one, just like the guy's own, her eyes focus on me with a sharpening intensity. It's almost as if she knows who I am just by looking at me.

She smiles, "Hey! Welcome to the neighborhood. My name is Deaton, and this is my wife, Alicia," he says, pointing to the woman.

I nod my head and stretch out my hand toward them. They both shake it. "Thanks, I'm Michael," still slightly uncomfortable with their preppy vibe.

"We know. We would have come over earlier to welcome you to the neighborhood, but we've been busy planning for the bonfire party tonight," Deaton says.

Alicia, who seems more grounded than her husband, chips in, "Also because we aren't the welcome committee," she is giving her husband a look that seems both chastising and loving, all at once. Deaton shrugs her comment off. "I take it you've met Lisa? She's the head of the welcome committee, and she mostly does the first greeting all by herself. She's the one who told us about you."

I nod. I have met Lisa. She came by the house yesterday. I think I still have a headache from her high-pitched voice and excessive giddiness. Thinking of Lisa's visit yesterday makes Alicia and Deaton look more normal. Is everybody here just so darn happy?

"Yeah, I've met Lisa." That's all I say.

Alicia nods, her eyes twinkling with amusement like she can hear what I am thinking, "Yeah, Lisa is the highest octave in our community."

Deaton smirks. I smile at Alicia and step back. "Please, come in," I say. Even though I feel it's against my better judgment to entertain the couple, something about them just seems so likable.

They enter, and as they look around the house, Deaton lets out a "Whoa!" Alicia slaps his arm, but I can see her eyes goggling at the size of the house.

"Man, you must be loaded," Deaton says, his eyes still roving all over the house.

I see Alicia's appalled look. Deaton must be the partner without the filter, I surmise. Alicia seems to be apologizing with her eyes. I shake my head slightly to indicate that it's fine.

Just then, Julia lets out a cry. Alicia and Deaton's eyes fasten towards the sound. I point towards the kitchen, where Julia is, in her stroller.

"I have to-," as I walk towards the kitchen. I hear Alicia and Deaton's footsteps as they follow me. I turn to them. "We were on our way out before you guys came. I was going to take her for a walk. She hasn't been outside today, I guess that's making her cranky."

Deaton is already bent at his waist, smiling down at Julia as I talked. Alicia looks at Julia, she smiles, and then she looks up at me over her husband's head. Her eyes seem to say 'Now, that's where the shadows in your eyes are from.'

I blink, confused, because it feels like she understands. Alicia just smiles. She pats her husband's arm.

"Come on, Deaton, let's leave father and daughter to their walk." She then turns to me, "You have a beautiful daughter."

I look at her, and I feel the genuineness in her words.

"Thank you," I say.

She nods. "You're welcome. Why we came here, actually, was to invite you to the bonfire party tonight. Everyone's going to be there. It would be a nice place to meet everybody. It starts at 10:00 p.m. We'll see you there. We have to go tell your next-door neighbors too."

Alicia nudges Deaton along, who is still smiling at Julia. He looks at me. "She is beautiful, man," he says and slaps me lightly on my arm. I smile. "Thanks."

Deaton must love babies. Something tells me they'll love him back too, Alicia says.

I nod to Alicia as they both turn to leave. I close the door behind them. I didn't even know I had a next-door neighbor.

Chapter 4

OLIVIA

Tuesday. 10:35 p.m.

I sip from my red cup as I look around the party. Music blasts from the speakers, and people- mostly middle-aged men and women, with the occasional seventy-somethings, laugh and chat with one another. Everybody seems to be having a great time. Which is a real puzzler. Bonfire parties, red cups, blasting music, these things are generally high school kids' forte. But it seems here in Catalina, the parents know how to have a good time too.

I smile as I drink from my cup again. I don't even know what I'm drinking, but it tastes good.

I hadn't even known about the 'hip' parents when I decided to vacation in Catalina. Nevertheless, it was a very nice bonus. Loud parties drown out sad thinking, and that is exactly what I need.

A tall blonde woman with a model-like figure walks past me, and my mind flashes to Marilyn. After she and her friends had left my shop on Sunday, I started making arrangements to travel to Catalina Island. It was like after knowing about the

Island, I couldn't wait to be here. The next day, I had gotten on a plane to take me there.

That was when I had texted Marilyn, telling her my assistant, Marjorie, would take care of her wedding cake and everything else. Her text back had not been pretty, but she hadn't been able to call back, because of flight mode. Yes, I had timed it just so.

I sigh and drink some more of my unnamed liquid. It's not like I hadn't baked the cake and other treats already. I had. Marjorie would just be in charge of making sure they got to the wedding venue in time. But, I still can't help feeling the little trickle of guilt I feel when I think of leaving Marilyn the way I did. After all, the first half of her wedding deserts payment was what paid for the house I was currently inhabiting on Catalina Island.

The house is... humongous. I use 'humongous' for both a lack of a better word, and also for its aptness. When I had contacted the agent- a drab woman by the way- and she had told me that it was the only house available, I almost felt my eyes pop out in shock from the price alone. Regardless, leaving, just leaving, had been a priority. So, I had taken the house.

I had used half my savings on booking the flight and kept the other half for anything I might need while I'm here. So, by the end of my 'vacation,' I will be broke, probably out of business due to the surely bad reviews that Marilyn would leave on my business website.

Yep, I'm living the dream.

I drink my mysterious liquid again. I feel my head swim, but I shake it off. Just then, I see Alicia and Deaton walking toward me. Earlier today, they had come over to my humongous house to invite me to the party. On seeing the inside of my house, Deaton had said something like 'Wow, you guys must be living in a garden of money.' I hadn't known who 'you guys' were, but I had snorted and said 'I wish' to the living in a garden of money bit. Deaton's unfiltered comment and Alicia's deep amusement had been endearing, and I had instantly liked them.

I smile now as they stop in front of me.

"Great party!" I shout to be heard over the loud music. Man, the music is loud!

Alicia and Deaton had both changed from their earlier clothes. And now, they are covered in bright and colourful clothes. Alicia's ears jingle with several earrings as she bounces on her feet to the music.

"Thanks!" she shouts back with the same large grin as earlier in the day.

"Don't you think the music is too loud? I feel like I'm in a teenager's rave!"

Alicia and Deaton look at each other and laugh. "That's exactly what we were going for."

Our boys think we can't have any fun, and this 'rave' is like a 'suck it' to their faces. When she sees I'm confused about the 'our boys' comment, she adds, "We have two teenage kids. Alex and Dylan."

My eyebrows go up. I look at the two drunk and colourfully-dressed adults in front of me. These two have teenage kids?

Alicia laughs at the look of utter disbelief on my face. "We get that a lot!"

I just shake my head. I knew I liked them for a reason.

"Hey!" Alicia waves at somebody. She turns to me, "Enjoy yourself!" she says. She takes Deaton's hand and drags him away.

As I watch them go, I walk over to the punch table. Yes, there is a punch table-this party was serious. Alicia and Deaton sure knew how to stick it to someone. I take the ladle and scoop up some pink liquid. I should be more careful about what I put in my stomach.

"I don't think you want to drink that," a voice beside me says.

I turn to look at the owner of the voice. And I have to look up, and as I do, I find myself looking into the greenest eyes I have ever seen in my life.

The party lights reflect over his face in swirling colours of red, blue, and green. The man has a full head of black hair, and his face is the most handsome face I had ever seen in my life. Not handsome in a soft kind of way, but hard planes and hard angles. And not too hard that they look scary. Everything seems balanced on his face, almost like God took extra time when designing him. His eyes, the greenest eyes, look down at me and I feel a tingle run up my spine. My eyes trail down to his mouth, his lips that look like they are meant for kissing. His nose is the right kind of nose for his face. Everything is just balanced.

His eyebrows go up, and I blink. I clear my throat.

"Oh, why?" I ask, as I remember his comment. I look down at the pink liquid in my cup.

The man shakes his head slightly. "That was the first thing I had when I came, and that was about thirty minutes ago. And I still don't feel right."

He places a hand on his stomach, his brows furrowing like he can't figure out what's going on in his stomach.

My eyes travel from his hand, to his- his thick, muscled arms, to his broad chest that spans and stretches in his shirt. I gulp as I feel another tingle run through me.

I put the cup to my lips, to hide my reaction to this man I barely know. The pink liquid touches my tongue, and I realize I like the taste of this one too. I drink it.

The man's eyebrows go up as he watched me drink.

Somehow, my eyes continue to stay on his, and he doesn't remove his from mine. The music from the party dims, and all I can hear is the roar of my heart beating in my chest.

Just then, somebody bumps into me, and the contact is broken. What was I doing having a strange connection between me and a man? I don't even know his name, but I feel exhilarated.

As if he can read my thoughts, the man says, "I'm Michael."

"Olivia," I say.

He nods. We both turn our backs to the punch table, to face the party.

"Alicia and Deaton sure know how to throw a party," Michael says.

"It's a 'suck it to their teenage kids' kind of party, two boys," I say.

The man, damn it, Michael, looks down at me, eyebrows raised. "Alicia and Deaton have kids?" he asks with disbelief coating his voice.

I laugh. "They get that a lot," mirroring how they answered me earlier.

The man smiles before turning to look out at the part once more. "Wow," he says, still trying to grapple the information.

That smile. My heart beats wildly as I struggle to recover from the effect of his blinding smile on me.

We don't talk for a while. The music and the party noise rave around us. Just then, the man's- crap- Michael's- when will I get his name stuck in my head- hand grazes mine. Just slightly. So slightly that I wouldn't even have noticed it if I wasn't hyper-vigilant of him beside me.

But I feel it. I look up at him; he's looking down at me. A delicious feeling rushes through me at the knowledge of what I see in Michael's eyes.

I already know what I'm going to do. Even as I continue to look into his eyes, I already know I am going to have sex with him. So, I have to at least know the name of the person I'm going to be going home with tonight.

Michael.

His name is the last thought in my mind before I close the distance between us, and press my lips to his. He meets mine halfway.

Chapter 5

MICHAEL

Wednesday. 8:15 a.m.

A thousand horses gallop through my brain. Or stampede, rather, seeing as it feels like there are almost a thousand freaking horses running up there. Their hooves dig in, and I fear the damage they will cause. But they are all in my head, so the raging headache currently roaring through my head is probably the worst it will get. I'm sure no horses are galloping through my head, but I swear that's what it feels like.

I press a bottle of cold water to my forehead and groan. *What the hell did I drink last night?* Scratch that. *What the hell was last night?*

I can't remember anything. I close my eyes and try to bring the events of last night to focus, but I can remember nothing. Absolutely nothing.

God. I sit straight on the kitchen stool and throw my head back. Maybe she'll remember more than I do.

I open my eyes and bring my head back straight. *She?* There was a woman? I look around the room. I'm the only one here. I know there's no one in my room because I came out of there just this morning.

I frown, trying again to bring last night to the forefront of my mind. And this time, I remember talking to someone at the party. I remember the person laughing. I remember standing beside them, looking out at the party, but the 'person' is just a black shape. I run a hand through my hair. But if the person were a woman... I try to picture the black shape as a woman. And I can see it. I get a vague image, and then it's gone.

"Damn it!"

My stomach growls, and I close my eyes. I don't have to look in the fridge to know there's nothing in the way of food there.

I shake my head. I am too old for this. Honestly.

I grab my phone from the counter and walk to Julia's room. A few minutes after they left my house yesterday, I got a call from Alicia. She had called to give me the number of a high school girl, Katie, who she had vouched was the best babysitter in the neighborhood. I had reservations, but when I had opened the door to a teenage girl with a gentle smile and brunette hair curling around her face like an angel, and- Julia had taken to her the moment she smiled at her, I had been convinced.

I sigh and pick Julia up from her crib. She smiles at me.

"We're going to the supermarket, Doc."

I push Julia's stroller as I walk down the aisle with shelves of booze. I wince.

29

"Yeah, Daddy is going to be regretting that for a long while," I whisper to Julia.

I walk a few steps and hear my name being shouted from behind me. I turn and find Alicia waving at me.

I frown slightly. She doesn't look like the person who hosted a wild rave the other night. She looks refreshed, her eyes are clear, and the smile she keeps smiling at me as she stops in front of me is just too wide for someone who should be having a hangover, like me.

Alicia bends at her waist to smile at Julia in her stroller.

"Hey, baby!" she croons to Julia. Julia smiles back at her, waving her little arms. Alicia's face brightens even more. "Oh! She is so precious. I have to carry her." So saying, she undoes Julia's safety belt and lifts her out of her stroller. She cradles her, doing silly faces that make Julia smile more.

I can't help it; I smile at the two of them. "Hello, Alicia. Man, how are you looking so.... okay, after last night? It feels like a marching band is playing in my brain. I think they are leaving, but I can still hear the echoes of their feet."

Alicia props Julia on her hip in that expert way of a woman who had done it more than a few times. She smiles at me. "Years of practice, Michael. Oh, Deaton would hate missing seeing cute baby Julia. I have to go and show her to him." She already starts pulling Julia's stroller before I can even talk.

I let go of the stroller and just smiled, resigned, as Julia waved her hands in obvious delight.

As Alicia leaves, she says, "Oh, funny coincidence, I saw Olivia by the pharmacy aisle just a minute ago. I saw you and her leave last night, if you want to say hi." Alicia leaves with Julia.

Olivia? The woman I left with, she's here. I look around the aisle where I'm standing. People walk about. The pharmacy aisle? Julia and I passed there a few minutes ago.

I trace my steps back, and a couple of aisles from the booze aisle, I get to the pharmacy aisle. People are going about their business here, too. My eyes track over them. I don't even know what, or who, I'm searching for looks like. I try to bring the color of her hair to my remembrance—Brunette, black- blonde. My eyes fix on a woman standing by one of the shelves. Her short blonde hair covers her face like a blanket as she looks down into her cart.

As I stand, still trying to figure out if she's the one I had gone with last night, she raises her head. She's wearing sunglasses inside the supermarket. She rubs a hand over her forehead and jumps when someone drops a skillet pan into their cart beside her.

I walk towards her, my strides purposeful. I walk around to stand in front of her. Her head is still down, and then slowly, she lifts her gaze. Her eyebrows furrow above the glasses as she looks up at me. Slowly, she removes her sunglasses, and as her hazel eyes focus on me, the memories slam into me.

I remember warning her about the punch. I almost scoff out loud at the irony, but the memories keep on slamming into me. I remember her laughter more clearly now. I remember the loud music clearly. It had been Imagine Dragons playing. And I remember when our fingers touched. Was I the one who made a move? And I remember our lips meeting.

I look at her lips now. Oh, I remember kissing those lips. I remember them muddling my brain and clouding my thoughts. I remember I hadn't been able to think while I was kissing them. I remember taking her hand and walking away from the party noise. Yeah, I made the first move there.

Now, I remember we had stopped a few feet away from the party. The noise level had reduced. I could still hear the people, but they were far away. The party had been on the beach, and there was a chaise lounge, obviously left by someone, where we stood. I remember looking at it and looking back at her, and she said, "It's fine." I remember having conflicted thoughts on that. Even one-night stands should have a little bit of finesse. I remember suggesting going to her place, but she had said, "No, it's better this way. We can each go to our houses after, make it less awkward when we wake up."

And then, because my head had been roaring with the need to keep kissing her pulsing through me, I nodded, and our lips met again. We had both fallen on the chaise lounge, and the memories of what we did after that slammed into me with crushing clarity.

"Oh God," I mutter.

Hands, teeth, blonde hair thrown back, mindless pleasure on her face. Moans, groans, total blindness to everything around me as I sink into her.

I look at her. She looks at me. People walk past us.

I stretch my hand out to her. "Hi, I'm Michael," I say.

She stares at my hand for a minute and looks up at me. I keep my eyes focused on hers. I shrug lightly. She smiles slowly, and I watch as it transforms her face.

She takes my outstretched hand. "Hi, I'm Olivia."

I smile. "Nice to meet you, Olivia. Permanent resident? Or visiting?"

"Visiting."

"Hmm, two visitors have a one-night stand in a place they don't know that well, and yet, they meet in the supermarket. What are the odds of that?"

She laughs. "Well, you have to give us props for our level of responsibility. That drunk, and we still knew it would not be good to go to either of our houses. That is pretty impressive," she says.

I do like it now that I'm thinking about it, and then I nod. "Yeah, it is pretty," I say.

She laughs again, and I think about how I like her laugh. But then, the thought is interrupted by Alicia's voice calling my name. I turn to see her walking towards me with Julia. I smile as she says, "I think Julia misses her Daddy."

I turn back to Olivia, still smiling. I see a look of utter shock on her face.

Chapter 6

OLIVIA

Wednesday. 8:45 a.m.

I had a one-night stand with a married man. No, not just married. A family man.

I look at his cute baby, she is smiling at me in that sweet way babies do. Except she's even sweeter. My chest tightens as I look into her eyes, her blue, wide, and beautiful eyes.

I can't smile back at her because I'm busy feeling waves of guilt crash into me.

I turn to her Daddy. Her handsome, mouth-watering.... no, no, no, Olivia. I shake my head. He is a father. And a husband. To some poor, poor, woman who didn't know what her husband was out doing last night.

"Hey, no, it's not what you think," he says, trying to clear the air.

I raise my eyebrows. He frowns, and a look.... like hurt.... pass across his face.

"I would never do that," he says.

Out of the corner of my eye, I see Alicia's eyes pass between the two of us. She then steps forward.

"Oh, no, this man right here is a single Dad. As handsome as they come too," she says and laughs, probably hoping to dispel the tension between us.

I look at her, then at the sweet baby, and finally, at Michael's still-hurt expression. I sigh.

"I'm sorry. I didn't mean to imply that...." I trail off because Alicia is still standing there, looking between the two of us.

After a minute of still tense silence, I look at Alicia. Pointedly, she blinks and starts. She clears her throat.

"Right. I should.... go," she says. She makes a vague gesture with her free hand. She gives the baby to Michael and aligns the stroller next to him.

I look at him again, and my heart clutches at the sight of him holding his baby to his chest.

"I'm sorry, again. I didn't mean to jump to conclusions like that," making sure my face reflects my apology.

He looks at me for a few seconds, and then he shrugs. "It's fine. I guess it's a logical conclusion."

"Yeah, but you didn't deserve it." We stand, looking at each other, and then the baby makes a babbling sound. My attention is turned to her. I smile, I just can't help it. She is the cutest baby I have ever seen. Not that I had seen a lot. "What's her name?"

"Julia," he says. He looks down at her in his arms, and I can see the pure look of love in his eyes. I almost feel embarrassed, because it feels like I'm peeking in on a private moment between father and daughter.

But it is all so cute, I just smile at them.

"So where was she last night?" I ask.

"Oh, she was at a rave too. Yeah, they had a theme, 'Nobody puts Baby in a corner,'" he says.

I look at him, and he has a straight look. My lips twitch, and I continue looking at him. He holds his straight face for an impressive minute, and then he grins.

"She was with a sitter. Katie. Alicia introduced her to me yesterday," he clarifies.

I nod, and with my face so straight, it's deadpan, I say, "Katie? I know Katie. I saw her at the party last night."

He was bending down to put Julie in her stroller as I talked. He pauses midway and looks up at me sharply.

"What?"

"Yeah. Sweet girl, that Katie. I think she had a drink of that pink thing you warned me about,"

He looks up at me, I keep on my straight face. When I see the muscle in his eye start to twitch, I smile again, slowly.

"Jesus," he says. He places Julia in her stroller, gently. He clicks the safety belt in place, and then stands up and looks at me. "Jesus," he says again. And then he starts laughing, almost without control.

I laugh too, almost unable to help myself.

After a while, he says, "That's mean. That is just plain mean."

I laugh some more. "I had to."

And then we start walking together. He pushed Julia's stroller, and I pushed my cart.

I see people looking at us with an 'aww' expression on their faces. My heart bumps nervously against my chest.

I hear a woman whisper to her partner as she walks past us. "Oh, look, honey, aren't they a cute family?"

I almost scoff out loud. As if. Just the knowledge of people admiring us as a family has my palms sweating.

I wipe my hand on my jeans.

"So, who are you visiting?" Michael asks.

"Uh?" I bring my thoughts back. I look up at him, and I blink. "Oh, yeah, I'm not visiting anybody. I'm vacationing," I say.

His face lights up in surprise. "Me too!"

I nod, smiling at him. "Oh really?" I block out the looks and whispers.

"Yeah. What do you do for a living?" Michael asks.

"Oh, I'm a Baker. I bake" I say awkwardly.

"Oh." Michael looks interested.

I nod. "Yeah. This vacation was sort of a desperate 'I-have-to-leave-town-like-right-now' type of vacation."

Michael scoffs lightly. "I know what you mean. Mine wasn't desperate, but I had to get out."

I tilt my head. "What do you do for a living?" I ask reciprocally.

Michael picks up a pack of spaghetti. He looks at me. "Can I?" he asks, holding up the pack of spaghetti and pointing it toward my cart.

"Oh." I hesitate. Shopping together doesn't mean living together. Get a grip, Olivia.

I smile. "Sure."

He drops the spaghetti inside my cart. "Thanks. Um, I'm a doctor," he adds, in answer to my question.

My eyebrows go up. "Wow. Impressive. What kind of doctor?"

"I'm an orthopaedic surgeon," he says.

"Wow." "So, you treat bones and stuff?"

He nods. "Yeah. But it wasn't the job that made me take the vacation."

He doesn't say anything after that, with no explanation for the comment, so I assume he doesn't want to talk about it.

"So, Julia's mom...." I trail off, because there's no way to ask a man about the mother of his child. A person who is so not in the picture. It's probably why questions like it were not commonly asked. Like, ever. Good going, Olivia.

I peer up at Michael, and I see that blank look; the same look he had had after not explaining the reason for taking the vacation. Lightbulb moment. Julia's mom is the reason for him taking the vacation.

I grimace. "Scratch that. I don't need to know. Even more, you don't need to talk about it."

Michael looks at me, and something passes through his eyes. Instead of acting on what I presume was a thought, he just nods and says nothing.

We walk for a while, saying nothing. Michael picks up a box of crackers; I pick up a box of butter. Michael picks up a pack of bacon; I pick up a block of yeast. Michael picks up noodles, cooking oil, and seasoning cubes, and I pick up flour, strawberry flavor, and salt. Michael picks up a pack of sugar, I pick up six.

His eyebrows go up.

I shrug. "Baker, remember? Sweet tooth guaranteed."

He smiles. My heart lifts as I see his smile. His smile says we are back to normal.

Back to normal? Taking out our night of insanity, I have only known Michael for this time we are spending together shopping, which is, what, 2-3 hours? When did we have time to have a 'normal' in that? And why am I happy because we are back to it? Like his happiness matters to me.

That nervous jump in my heart happens again. I look down at Julia in her stroller to steady myself. That was a mistake, because her sweet baby face and those blue eyes that are looking up at me make my heart constrict even more. I feel my chest squeeze, cutting off my air.

"Hey, you okay?" Michael asks, looking at me with concern.

I look up at him and give him a shaky smile. "Yeah, I'm fine."

He doesn't look convinced, but he nods, and we walk toward the checkout counter.

I peer down at Julia again. Why do I feel like I've known those eyes forever?

EMMA LENA

We are now outside the supermarket. Michael hoists his bag of groceries in one arm and pushes Julia's stroller with his other hand. He walks towards a white RAV4 car and presses a button, opening the booth of the car. Seeing him struggle to balance both the button, his groceries, and his baby gives my heart that little bump again. He deposits the bag of groceries in the trunk and then closes it.

He turns and gives me a wary smile. I wave at him, and then at Julia.

I watch as he arranges Julia into the car seat, and gets in himself. I stand and watch as he drives off.

Chapter 7

MICHAEL

One week later. Wednesday. 5:30 p.m.

"Yeah, Marie, I'll let my four-month-old baby know you said 'hello.'" I smile wryly as Marie's voice filters in through the phone's speaker.

Marie Mason, a 50-something-old woman, one of the nurses in the hospital I work at was back at home. The most interesting thing about Marie, aside from her fascinatingly bright sweaters, is her blatant obliviousness to sarcasm. She just never seems to get it, and somehow, that makes her my favorite nurse.

My friend and colleague, Jack Baldwin, a Radiologist, called me this morning. He called to catch up on how much I'm enjoying my vacation. I guess Marie had been there, and now we'd been on the phone for the past forty-five minutes.

"Okay, Marie, I have to go now. Yes, all right, bye-bye now." I finally cut the call, and I look at Julia. She is in her stroller, staring wide-eyed at me. "Yeah, so, that was Marie. She says hi." Julia just stares right back at me, unblinking. "I told her you'd say that,"

The doorbell rings.

I stand up and walk to the door. I open it to find Deaton on the other side. His friendly face lights up as he smiles.

"Hey man! How's it going?"

"Not bad. What's up?" I ask.

"Oh, it's nothing much," he says. He is already walking over the threshold, so I have to step aside.

"Come in," I mutter, closing the door behind him.

He walks to the living room like he has been living in my house for ages.

"Alicia is at the hospital, so I'm kind of bored. I came over to greet princess Julia. Hey, Julia!" He walks over to Julia's stroller, his face alight with pleasure, and crouches down so their eyes are level. He is already playing silly faces with her. I'm still confused over his first statement.

"Wait, Alicia is in the hospital? Is she okay?"

"Hmm?" Deaton says, distracted, as he continues playing with Julia. And then, he seems to click with my question. "Oh, no, not *in* the hospital. *At.* She's a doctor there. A Physiotherapist."

My eyebrows go all the way up. "Alicia is a doctor?" I ask.

"Mmhmm," Deaton says, now tickling Julia. Suddenly, he turns to me. "Hey, here's an idea, let's all go over to the hospital. Yeah, I bet Alicia will be stoked to see Julia."

I'm already shaking my head. I'm a doctor, so I know how crazy the work can be. As much as I love Julia, I prefer to have my mind completely focused on work when I'm in the hospital.

"I don't think Alicia would appreciate us crashing in on the workplace like that."

Deaton waves me off. "Oh, it's fine. I work there too. The hospital's hardly crazy this time of the evening," he says nonchalantly.

I have the second shock of the evening. "You're a doctor too?"

He looks at me like it should be obvious. "Yeah, I am a Cardiologist."

Wow. I shake my head, trying to clear the surprise Deaton's words are bringing me.

"I've never seen doctors party the way you guys did last week." Still surprised by the fact that the man who is wearing a sweater with a mixture of yellow, wine-red, blue, white, and black, and who is currently sticking his tongue out playfully at a baby, is a doctor.

Deaton lifts Julia out of her stroller. She babbles happily. "Hey, in my opinion, doctors should be the most appreciative of life. We see the other side way too much- not to be," he says, rocking Julia in his arms. He cocks his head slightly towards the door. "Now, come on, let's go see Alicia."

Since he was already walking towards the door with my child, I have no choice but to grab my keys from the kitchen counter and follow him.

Five minutes later, we pull up in front of Catalina Island Medical Center. It looks more like a house than a hospital. There are shrubs lined in front of the building, and a few steps lead up to the entrance.

Deaton releases Julia's car seat and lifts her out of the car. He carries her in her car seat towards the building, and I follow. As we enter, the first thing I notice, because it just kind of jumps right out at me, is the calming ambiance of the hospital. There are calls for doctors to rooms, and few patients and visitors milling about like any other hospital, but there just seems to be a calming presence to it all.

There is a medical receptionist at the front desk, she looks up and her face lights up with pleasure as she sees us. Or rather, Deaton. Or maybe it's Julia, because her eyes are trained on Julia's car seat, and she's almost falling out of her seat, hoping to catch a glimpse of the baby.

Does everybody just love babies here?

She looks to be in her mid-thirties. She is a bright redhead, with a short wavy cut, and tiny dots of freckles scattered on her nose.

"Hey, Rocky! I brought us a bundle of cuteness to brighten our day here," Deaton says, gently placing Julia's car seat on the counter.

I look at her name tag, and her name is, indeed, Rocky.

Rocky smiles into Julia's car seat and makes cooing noises. "Hey, Julia! Oh, you are a very beautiful baby," she whispers to Julia.

"I know, right?" Deaton says, smiling like he just won a prize. "This is her dad, Michael," he taps me on my shoulder.

Rocky looks up at me, she stretches her hand out. "Hi! I'm Rocky."

I nod and shake her hand. "Nice to meet you."

Her eyes take on a speculative glint. "Vacationing?" she asks.

"Yeah. The island is a beautiful place."

A warm look joins the speculation in her eyes, and she nods. "That it is. You here with anybody, or...." she trails off.

"Oh, no, he's here solo," Deaton says before I can reply. "Okay, let's go see Alicia now," he picks up Julia's car seat, and waves goodbye to Rocky.

I give Rocky a small smile before following Deaton. She smiles back and gives a small wave as we go, I feel her speculative eyes on me as I walk away.

We go down a hallway, pass rooms with patients with nurses in some and patients with their visitors in others. We turn a corner to the right; I see an office with the door ajar, and I physically shudder at the fact that someone would invite that kind of crazy in willingly. And then Deaton enters the office, and says, "Hey honey! Look who came to grace your office with her presence."

I enter, and I see Alicia seated behind the large desk in the office.

"Of course..." I mutter to myself, as I start to put my metaphorical foot into my metaphorical mouth.

Alicia is already up, and out of her chair, smiling at Julia, even as I fully enter the room.

By the end of Alicia's shift at 7:00 p.m., I had been given the play-by-play of the hospital's activities. They had Cardiologists, Radiologists, Physiotherapists, Family Medicine, and some other practices, but no Orthopaedic treatment. Additionally, they had great reviews on their website.

I turn to Alicia, halting our steps as we get to the entrance of her office from the tour of the hospital.

My brows furrow as a suspicious thought comes to my mind. "Are you trying to tell me something here, Alicia?"

She looks up at me with an innocent look on her face. "What do you mean?"

My eyes narrow. "I'm only here for vacation. Six months. That's all. I have a job back at home."

Alicia shrugs, her eyes trailing away from mine. She walks into her office, and I follow her.

"It's just something to think about, that's all." she says with a mischievous glint in her eyes.

I sigh. I lean against a cabinet. "I am not going to be living here, Alicia. This was just meant to be a break of some sort. For me, and Julia."

"I know, I know. But, you could live here. I mean, you like it here, right? These past couple of weeks has been great? I know it has, 'cause Deaton and I have been at your place almost every day."

I look at her. "You don't even know my work history. You don't even know if I'm that good at my practice."

"We called your workplace and requested your file. You are very good, and you know it, Doctor Rosenbaum."

"You called my...." I sigh again. The call today from Jack suddenly made a whole lot of sense.

Alicia walks over to me and lays a hand on my arm. Those shrewd eyes of hers that had pierced through me the first time I met her, looking into mine now.

"Look, I don't know what made you take a vacation in the first place, but I have a feeling whatever it is- it hurts. Catalina Island has a way of healing hurts. You just have to give her a chance."

Chapter 8

OLIVIA

Friday. 8:30 a.m.

I open my eyes. I stare at the ceiling. I'm on my bed, and I am just waking up. It feels as though I haven't seen the sun in 237 hours. Days have blended into weeks. Weeks into months. Months into years. Years into centuries. And now I feel myself losing my grip on sanity.

I sigh. Of course, none of that is true. Well, except for the last part 'cause I am, indeed losing my sanity. Out of boredom. I can feel it. And I tend to get dramatic when I'm bored. That's why I'm thinking like I'm in a Lost episode.

I rub a hand over my face and stand up from my bed. It's been a week, give or take a few days, since the bonfire party, and I have been slowly losing my mind because of boredom. I know there are a gazillion things I could be doing. I have gone to the beach and soaked up the sun, kayaked- something I had never done before, and will never do again, surfed- I enjoy, and yet, something's missing. My shoulder blades are itching like there's something else I want to do.

I walk into my ginormous kitchen, in my ginormous house. I don't think I'll ever get used to this house. That I paid for, with my money.

I go to the fridge and open it. I start bringing out baking ingredients for donuts. Also, I have been baking for the past week. From cakes to pies to donuts. I mean, one would think I wouldn't have time to be so bored.

I stop bringing stuff out of the fridge as I realize there is no sugar left. I sigh. Sugar's the first ingredient that always finishes in my fridge. That's why I make sure to buy more than enough of it. I bought six packs of it that day, didn't I?

I smile to myself as the memory of Michael's face when I had bought six packs of sugar, comes to my head. Michael. I hadn't seen him for the past week either. One would think we would have crossed paths, maybe at the beach, or something. He did say he was here on vacation, right? What else do vacationers do in a place like Catalina Island, if not things like kayaking, surfing, and laying on the beach?

I bring my thoughts back to baking. Well, now I'm in the mood to bake. I don't want to go all the way to the supermarket for just sugar. My eyes go over to my screen door, I see the other ginormous house beside mine. Maybe they'll have sugar.

I press the bell to the ginormous house. I hear nothing for a minute, and then I hear the sound of footsteps. Seconds later, the door opens, and I find myself staring into the greenest eyes I have ever seen.

He is less shocked than I am because he is able to find his voice before I do.

"Olivia?" his brows are furrowed, and his beautiful face is twisted in surprise.

I finally find my voice. "You live here?"

"Yeah. How do you....?"

"I'm your next-door neighbor." I am starting to notice how delicious he looks. He is wearing a white undershirt on gray sweatpants, and his hair is all tousled like he was just running his hands through them. I want to run my hands through them.

I blink away the wayward thought and bring my mind back to reality as I realize he's saying something.

"...how did we not know?"

I shrug. "Beats me." Assuming he was asking how we didn't know we lived beside each other all along.

He steps aside like he just remembered I am still standing outside.

"Come in."

"Thanks." Then my breath whooshes out of me as I look around Michael's house. "Whoa," I breathe the word, "Yours is even more ginormous than mine."

"Ginormous?" he says.

I hear the amusement in his voice. I turn around to look at him. "This doesn't freak you out? You won't find this house at all intimidating?"

He looks at me, confused. "Should I?"

I cock my head. "Oh, of course, you don't. You're a surgeon. Surgeons roll around in this type of money." I walk to the kitchen, and my eyes bulge at the spaciousness of it. "Wow," I run my hand over the smooth panel of the kitchen countertop. I turn to Michael. "Where is Julia?"

He is standing by the entrance to the kitchen. He crosses his arms together. "Oh, she's sleeping. She wakes up in the middle of the night, cries, and then goes back to sleep till a few minutes before nine." He looks at the time on his phone. "She should be waking up anytime now."

"Oh," I nod my head, still looking around the kitchen.

"What did you come here for in the first place?" he says.

I turn my attention back to him. "Oh, right! Yeah, I was going to ask if you had sugar. I wanted to bake, and I didn't have any sugar left, so.... but I know you probably wouldn't have any, I mean, you only bought one pack that day."

Michael's eyebrows go up. You don't have any sugar left? You bought six packs that day," clearly incredulous at my rate of sugar intake.

I feel a flush ride up my neck. I shrug. "Well, I have been baking almost every day. I told you, sweet tooth guaranteed."

Michael chuckles. "Wow," he walks past me to his fridge, which is also bigger than mine. He tosses a pack of sugar, with just a little use out of it.

I catch it and I recognize it as the brand of sugar we had both bought that day. "You haven't used up your one pack?" I ask incredulously.

Michael shrugs and smiles. My heart skips a beat at his smile, the way it makes his whole face lighter. I suddenly feel self-conscious standing in his kitchen with him, I'm wearing a pink top that says, BAKE- in big bold black letters, and black sweatpants. No bra. My hair is up in a messy ponytail, and I'm standing in front of the most beautiful man I have ever seen.

I start to retreat. "Um, I have to go. Got lots.... to bake," I finish lamely.

Michael's brows furrow. "Oh, come on now, you can take a few minutes before you have to start, right? Come on, let me give you a tour", he tilts his head in a come-ahead gesture.

Since he's already walking, I follow him.

"This is the living room, where we catch up on Doc McStuffins on Disney, and all her friends," Michael says.

I smile. What's more appealing than a successful man with a hot gorgeous body? Answer; a successful man with a hot gorgeous body and a cute little girl that he adores to pieces.

"Here is the guest room, which has been used as Alicia and Deaton's dump site for the past week for their teenage son's birthday presents."

"Oh, one of their son's birthdays is coming up soon?" I ask.

"Yeah, the younger one, Alex. They're having a little cookout in their backyard tomorrow. You should come," he says, turning slightly to look at me.

"Oh, I don't know. They didn't invite me, and I don't want to crash their party or anything like that."

Michael looks at me. "Really? Alicia and Deaton? Have you met those two? You know it's the more the merrier with them. Those two are party animals." When he sees that I am not quite convinced, he adds, "Okay, how about this? We'll go together. You'll be my plus one. Uh?"

"I think Julia is already your plus one," I say.

We walk out to a terrace at the back of the house. It is lined with pots of flowers. I don't know much about flowers, but the arrangement is so beautiful. I fall in love with the terrace as I step onto it. There are a couple of relaxing chairs, with a small table in their midst.

"Oh, Julia is not a plus one, trust me. She's the major guest of the party," Michael says.

I cock my head. "Shouldn't that be the birthday boy?"

Michael leans on the terrace gate. "You would think," he says wryly.

Behind him, the waves from the beach lap over each other. Just a few feet away is where the bonfire party had taken place last week, and where we had had our night together.

My eyes trail to Michael, and he has this look in his eyes like he knows exactly what I'm thinking about. Like he's thinking about it too.

His voice is low and gravelly as he says, "Come on, say you'll go."

I can't seem to take my eyes off his, I feel a tingle at the base of my fingertips. "I'll go."

Just then, we hear Julia's waking cry.

Chapter 9

MICHAEL

Monday. 9:00 p.m.

"I just don't think you can put Joey on Michael Scott's level of dumbness. I mean, come on! (*inserts rolling eyes emoji)"

As I read Olivia's text, I'm on my bed, and the only light in the room is from my phone screen. And I'm smiling like an idiot.

The current argument is on who's dumber; Michael Scott from The Office, or Joey Tribbiani from Friends.

In my opinion, one can't determine the level of each of these characters' dumbness, mainly because they veer off in totally different, and specifically unique to their characters, brands of dumbness. But, I'm enjoying chatting with Olivia.

"Oh, come on, Jenkins, open your eyes here."

I send her a clip from Friends where Joey gets into his and Chandler's entertainment unit and allows himself to be locked in, just to show a completely random stranger that a person could fit into it. Leaving said random stranger free to do whatever he wants with all of the stuff in the living room.

"(*inserts five laughing emojis) Okay, Joey is not very bright."

"Oh really? I hadn't noticed."

"He's just so cute though! (*inserts cute eyes emoji) How you doin'?!"

"Okay, never, ever, again. That's Joeys', and Joeys' alone."

"Yes sir. (*inserts peace sign emoji)"

"You use too many emojis, btw."

"Bite me, Rosenbaum."

I smile again.

It's been three days since I and Olivia both found out we lived near each other. Even though that acknowledgement should have naturally turned us into those types of neighbors that practically live in each other's houses.... it hasn't.

Ever since the day we found out, we haven't been to each other's houses. Olivia had taken the sugar with her to her house. I stayed back at mine. A few hours later, she had dropped off some of the donuts she had baked, with the added note of telling me she had accepted my offer to go with me to Alicia and Deaton's son, Alex's birthday. She hadn't come in, and I hadn't invited her in.

I tasted her donuts, and found out her donuts were the best donuts I had ever eaten in my entire life. Albeit they had been a little bit too sugary for my taste.

We chatted on the phone that night and went together to the birthday party the next day. There had been a lot of whispering (some, a little too loud to be called that) by Alicia and Deaton's friends about whether or not we were going out. And we had kind of rolled with it. We didn't even say anything, we just kind of agreed silently with the ones who actually came up to us and asked us straight out.

Olivia had finally been convinced her- not getting an invite to the party was not an issue when Alicia hugged her excitedly as soon as she saw her walk into the party. Deaton had also said they came over to her place a couple of times to invite her, but she wasn't home.

We had left the party at around 8:00 p.m. as Julia's lids were already dropping in fatigue. Olivia waved goodbye to Julia in her car seat, mouthed 'text me,' and went on to her house.

We had chatted that night too, for four hours. We had finally gone to sleep around 12:30 a.m. the next day.

We chatted the next day after that. And then today.

"Favorite character from The Office. Go."

"Jim. Definitely."

"Of course. Go for the handsome laidback guy."

"Oh, please, like you wouldn't go for the cute receptionist, Pam."

"I find that offensive. My favorite character was Stanley."

*"(*inserts numerous laughing emojis) Bull. Shit. Bullshit, Rosenbaum."*

I send a gif of Michael shrugging, with his 'that's just me' look.

And she sends a gif of Stanley doing his 'I don't believe a word you say' face.

I grin stupidly.

Just then, I hear Julia's cry from her room. I have a baby monitor on my night-stand, but I also kept my bedroom door open, mainly because I don't fully trust the monitor, so I hear her cry loud and clear from her room.

I stand up and make my way to her room.

"Hey, Doc, what are the symptoms?" I croon as I go near her crib. She just lets out another wail. "Okay, so, just the wails then. I got you." I lift her out of her crib and start to bounce her gently in my arms. "I got you."

I walk back to my room, bouncing Julia in my arms. I see there is an unread text on my phone. I pick it up and read.

"Hey, sore loser, where'd you go?"

Typing with one hand, I reply.

"'Sore loser?' What'd I lose at?"

*"I don't even know. (*inserts monkey covering face emoji)."*

"Tsk tsk."

"Lol. Seriously. Everything okay?"

"Oh yeah, Julia just woke up crying. I'm bouncing her as we speak."

"Oh. Is she okay?"

I look at Julia, who is now slipping back into blissful sleep mode, her eyelids dropping.

"Yeah, she's fine. My girl just likes to have her own little 'queen of the whole wide world' moment at random times of the night. She's back to sleeping now."

"Okay."

The bubbles that indicate the other person typing, pop up. And then it clears. It pops us again. It clears again.

My brows furrow.

"Give her a kiss for me."

I stare at my phone for a beat. And then I kiss Julia on her forehead.

"Done."

"Thanks."

"No problem."

I feel like we had just gone through a kind of moment, and I am not even sure what the moment is. But I know I'm not ready for my chat with Olivia to end.

I settle on my bed to be more comfortable and rest against my headboard. I type around Julia's sleeping body.

"You watch Community?"

"Yes."

"Favorite character from Community. Go."

Five hours later. 2:30 p.m.

Michael's dream.

Nine months earlier.

I rub the back of my neck, trying to relieve myself of the tension. I had just completed a seven-hour surgery. Now, eighteen-year-old Taylor Roberts gets to start her journey of recovery from the life-threatening kneecap injury she had sustained five months ago in a car crash. She gets to finish college, get her creative writing degree, and publish her novel that she had been too nervous to submit before the accident.

I did that. My job is demanding, stressful, and time-consuming, but, God, at times like these, it's freaking awesome.

"Good job, Dr. Rosenbaum," Marie greets me.

She had assisted in the surgery, and while on other days, I would indulge her by staying and catching up with her on the latest hospital gossip, I am just too beat to do that now.

I slowly start to back away. "Thanks, Marie. You did a great job in there too."

She waves at me, and I wave back. I turn around before I see the next words forming on her lips.

I walk briskly down the hallway to my office. I open the door and enter, leaning against the door as I close it, and lock it. I turn around, and I'm startled to find Laura sitting in the visitor's chair.

"Jeez. Laura." I chuckle. And just like it always does anytime I see Laura, my heart warms with pleasure. I smile. "Miss me?"

She is wearing a silk cream-coloured shirt and a black pantsuit. She was supposed to have a job interview with a fancy, big-name, illustration company today. It was a really big deal for her. She had almost bounced with nervous energy this morning before she left, and Laura never bounced.

She gives me a small smile, but even with her obvious struggle to put on a brave face, I see immediately that something is wrong.

I go to her and crouch in front of the chair so our eyes are level. "Did the interview not go well?"

She shakes her head, and I see she's trying not to cry. I know Laura, I give her time to get out what's on her mind.

After a few seconds, she says, quietly, so much so I barely hear her, "I'm pregnant."

It takes me a few seconds; first to hear what she said, then to process the words, then to feel them in my heart, bursting into streams of joy.

My face spreads to a wide smile. "You're pregnant?" I whisper, afraid I'll somehow jinx the moment by being too loud. I bring Laura's face up with my hands, so I'm staring into her beautiful eyes. "We're having a baby?"

She nods. Then tears fill her eyes.

A part of me is bursting with pride and joy and love, all at once, at the news that I only perceive as the best news ever. But the other part of me, the part that is looking into Laura's eyes and seeing the opposite of the things I'm feeling, in them, sinks.

Chapter 10

OLIVIA

Tuesday. 10:00 a.m.

I walk into the auditorium. Well, the auditorium is maybe too big a word for it, it's more like a small-town meeting hall. There are rows of chairs arranged in columns of two, facing a small stage.

"You stalking me now, Jenkins?"

I turn around, and my heart gives a little jump (which I ignore) as I see Michael standing behind me.

I smile. "In your dreams, Rosenbaum," I say.

He looks good. But then again, for the past month in which I've known him, and the few times I've met him in person, he always looks good.

Today, he is wearing a gray wool sweater with a little bit of the white undershirt he wore underneath showing at his neck, over a pair of jeans. His hands are in the pockets of the jeans, and his hair is ruffled slightly, probably from the wind outside. His green eyes twinkle with amusement as he looks down at me.

I somehow manage to find my voice. "Julia?" I ask.

"Katie's babysitting her. Yeah, I think she might want to go home with her after today. They looked like they were best friends when I left."

I chuckle. "What are we doing here?" Alicia had called me yesterday and told me to come over to the hall today, without really giving me any details. I had been about to ask her what it was all about when she yelled something about 'maiming Dylan if he didn't get his backpack off the damn floor'. So, I had assumed she had to go, even before she said 'Sorry, Olivia, I have to go'.

And now, here I am.

Michael looks around the hall, the same as me. He shrugs. "Beats me. But while we wait for Alicia or Deaton, to find their way to us, and explain what we're doing here... Britta.... really?"

I shrug, already smiling. "What?"

"Britta Perry, *Buzzkill*, is your favorite character in Community. Are you kidding me, Jenkins?!" Michael shakes me a little, like he's trying to shake some sense into me.

I laugh. "She is not a buzzkill. She brings up really important issues, fights for women's rights, and is just generally a very passionate activist..." I cut off, and laugh again as Michael mock snores. I slap his arm playfully. "Stop it."

I'm just saying. Abed Nadir is there, Troy Barnes is there, hell, Shirley, is there! Oh, and Jeff. I mean."

I cock my head at him. "Oh, now who's going for the handsome laidback guy?"

He shakes his head at me like I'm a lost cause, just as Alicia and Deaton walk up to us.

"Hey guys!" Alicia smiles at us, "Glad you could make it."

"Yeah. 'It' being...?" Michael asks.

"Oh, yeah, we're throwing a carnival party on Step Beach, and we, the people in this room, are the party-planning committee. Isn't that fun?!"

My eyebrows go up at the enthusiasm in Alicia's voice. How many parties do these people have in a year?

Michael and I exchange a look.

"Well, I don't know exactly how I would be of help to you. I've never really planned a party before or been on any type of party-planning committee. So...."

Deaton waves Michael's comment off. "Oh, don't worry about that. I'm sure there are plenty of things we can find for you to do." He turns to me and smiles brilliantly. "Now you, you have a specific assignment."

Alicia smiles as her husband talks. I look between the two of them, at a loss as to what they are talking about.

"We read about your bakery, HEARTFILLED, on your bakery's website. All your treats just look so amazing!" Alicia says.

Deaton nods vigorously. "Yes, and we just have to have them! You're gonna bake them for us, for the carnival. What do you say?"

The two of them look at me with twin expressions of wide-eyed excitement and glee. Out of the corner of my eye, I notice Michael looking at me with interest.

"Sure," I whisper like there was a choice.

I smile and hug Alicia back as she hugs me, squealing happily.

"Great!", Deaton says. "We'll start the briefing soon, so sit tight."

He and Alicia wave, and walk away to talk with some other people.

I turn slowly back to Michael.

"So, a bakery. Fancy," he says.

I smile. "Yeah. HEARTFILLED. My pride and joy."

Michael gives me a look. Probably because of the way I said the 'pride and joy' like it was anything but. I don't know why I said it like that either.

"That's impressive. I think, even with your poor choice of character favorite in Community, I think I can bear to look at you. Just because of your bakery."

"Wow, thank you. For tolerating me," I say with sarcasm dripping from my voice.

"You're welcome," Michael says.

I laugh and Michael smiles at me. We both look at the hall. People are starting to take their seats, and the hall is now more filled than it was at the beginning.

"So, any more secrets you're not been telling me, Jenkins?" He pauses and looks around the room one more time. He looks down at his shoes. "Boyfriends, maybe. Serious relationships," he says the last part with a smile.

I smile back. I know he's trying to play the question off as a teasing one, but I hear the seriousness underneath it. And I know what it means.

My heart trips wildly in my chest. I try to match his light tone as I scoff. "Yeah right. Marilyn freaking Monroe knows I can't keep a boyfriend."

Michael's eyebrows go up in question. I shrug it off, slightly embarrassed.

"It's a long story. But, in answer to your question, no, I don't have a boyfriend or serious relationship back at home."

Michael looks down at me, a look passes in his eyes. It's so brief, it's gone before I can blink.

65

He just nods. "Cool."

I nod too. "Cool."

Two hours later, we stand up from our chairs and clap as Alicia rounds up the first official carnival party-planning committee meeting.

People disperse into groups. There had been whispers today too, just like at Alex's birthday party. From the little I had gleaned from the ones that were, once again, a little too loud to be called whispers, they had concluded I and Michael were going out.

Michael must have heard them too, 'cause he had looked at me at the same time I had heard them, smiled at me, and held his hands out in a 'what can you do' gesture.

We follow most of the crowd to the table in a corner of the hall, where food was laid out in different delicacies.

We look over at Alicia, a few feet away from us, as she laughs at something someone says to her. Deaton is beside her, and he grabs her arm and laughs loudly too.

"And just to think, those two are doctors," Michael says.

I look up at him in surprise. I didn't know this. "They are?"

Michael nods his head. "Hmm-hmm. Alicia is a physiotherapist, and Deaton's a cardiologist. They both work over at the Catalina Island Medical Center."

"Wow," truly surprised. I look over at them again. They are now clinging to each other like newlyweds.

"I mean, I'm a doctor, right, and I've never seen doctors look that happy. Our work is stressful, and more often than we'd like, borders on the depressing part of life. So, there's usually scarce place left for joy, and parties." Michael shakes his head, looking at Alicia and Deaton. "But these two, they make it work. Somehow, they find happiness in life, even amidst all the pain. That's one hell of a skill."

"Yeah. I bet," I say, seeing a new side of Michael I haven't seen before. The doctor's side. It makes me wonder about all the death, and pain, he must see in his work. Then I wonder how it has changed his way of thinking, his way of looking at life.

Was that why he loved his little girl so fiercely? Because when you see that much death, it makes you appreciate life more.

Suddenly, Michael looks down at the spread of food on the table, and he grins. I blink, dazzled by the transformation the grin brings to his face. I look down at the table too. I look back up at him, puzzled.

"What?" I ask.

"Nothing. It's just, this is quite the spread," Michael says.

"Yeah, it is," still not seeing what he was grinning about.

He lifts a pan of pie. "And nobody's eating any of it. We shouldn't let it go to waste, Alicia and Deaton must have spent a fortune."

A suspicious feeling runs through me as I look at the playful glint in Michael's eyes.

"Michael," like a warning.

And that's the last thing I say before the pan of the pie goes splat on my face.

"Food fight!"

Chapter 11

MICHAEL

8 months ago. 6:15 p.m.

I rub my hands together. I am nervous, excited, and restless, all at once. Imagining the different ways the evening could go has me strung out in different directions.

I fiddle with one of the candles on the bookshelf. Maybe I shouldn't put a lit candle next to books, I think to myself. I carry the three candles away from the bookshelf. I look around the room, most of the flat surfaces in the room already have candles on them. Maybe the candles are too much. Yeah, they're too much.

I blow out the candles in my hand, I go into the kitchen and put them in one of the cupboards there.

I am at Laura's house, waiting for her to come home from the supermarket. She hadn't gotten the job she interviewed for a month ago at the big-name illustration company. The company had wanted to go on tour for a new manga series they had just put out, and they had been looking for a fresh new illustrator who could develop ideas for their new manga series that they planned to release during the tour. Because of the pregnancy, three months along on the day of the interview when she had found out, Laura had not been able to go for the job.

She had been down for the past month, seeing as she had been looking forward to working with the company.

I have tried to be there for her and the baby. My work hours are as crazy as ever, but I make it a point of a conscious effort to make more time for Laura. I know about the effects of pregnancy hormones on women, and the high probability of it leading to depression. Add in Laura's feeling of sadness over losing her dream job, and she needs someone to be there for her even more.

Two weeks ago, I had done a rash thing. I proposed.

Sometimes, when I think back to that night, I still can't believe I did that. And sometimes, like now, I understand why I did.

We had been sitting in this same living room, relaxing. My head had been on Laura's lap, and we had been munching on popcorn as we watched one of Laura's favorite series, a show I had had no clue about and had teased Laura about mercilessly. It was one of those rare relaxed and happy moments that we scarcely had ever since we found out about the pregnancy, and I guess the moment had gotten to me.

One of the characters on the show had gotten down on his knee, and proposed to another character I assumed was his girlfriend. I had made a funny comment about the scene, Laura had laughed. And the next thing I know, I was on a bended knee, and I had taken Laura's hands out of the popcorn bowl and held them. I looked into her eyes, and said "Will you marry me, Laura?"

She had laughed, of course. I had laughed too; half-sure I was joking. And then I realized that I was completely one-hundred-percent serious. Just like that.

I wasn't laughing anymore. Laura had stopped laughing too when she saw my face, what was in my eyes. I had said it again, this time, with more seriousness;

"Marry me, Laura." Laura's hand had gone still in mine, and then she had whispered, brokenly; "No."

I had been shocked, as any guy who just had his proposal rejected would be. But then, later that night, we talked about it. And I had seen the 'craziness of it', as Laura had put it. Later, as we lay in bed, with Laura already asleep, I wondered if I had only seen the craziness in my proposal because Laura did. And I wondered because, with Laura asleep and left alone with my thoughts, I didn't find it so crazy after all.

Now, I fiddle with the bouquet of roses (Laura doesn't really like flowers. She tolerates roses). Now, I'm pretty sure it's not crazy at all. And this time around, I've thought this through for longer than the duration of a movie.

I hear the click of the door turning. I take a deep breath just as Laura enters the room.

She is four months along now, and though it barely shows yet, my eyes automatically go to the little mound of her protruding belly. Laura tries to cover it as much as she can with baggy sweaters and tops, but I already love the little human being growing in her, so much.

Laura's brows furrow, and she narrows her eyes as she looks around the room. At the lit candles, the petals of roses scattered on the floor, little cut-outs of character babies on the center table (a bit overkill, I know, but I don't plan to play fair, so I'm pulling out all the big guns). Low-key soft music plays in the background.

Because I know Laura, I wait for her to process.

She steps forward, her eyes on me now. "What is this? Michael," she says my name in a whisper.

When she stops in front of me, I take both her hands in mine.

"This is not craziness. Not this time. Marry me, Laura," looking into her eyes.

Her eyes track once more over the room. She looks back at me. "Michael," she says my name again, still in a whisper.

My eyes remain steady on hers. "I love you, Laura. I know we don't say it, but I also know we feel it. You love me." This I do not doubt about. "I love you so much it hurts. And now, I love this baby more than life itself. I want the two of you, I want both of you in my life. I want to take care of you, protect you, and provide for you. I want to be your husband. I want us to be a family in every sense of the world, in every way possible. Marry me, Laura."

I see tears fill up in her eyes, and I know I've won the war. There are still battles, even now, I can see them in her eyes, but I have won the war.

She shakes her head slightly. "Michael," she says in a whisper again.

I lean in, and close my lips over hers, silencing the battles.

We separate, and we look into each other's eyes. Laura leans in and kisses me again.

Present day. Thursday. 9:05 a.m.

I spray my favorite cologne lightly over my shirt as I look at my reflection in the mirror. I had just finished showering, and now wearing a blue checkered button-down shirt, with the buttons undone, over a white undershirt, and a pair of black jean trousers.

I'm planning on going over to Olivia's house. Alicia and Deaton have Julia for the whole day. They had insisted. And after talking myself out of it, and into it, more than a couple of times, I have finally decided to just go over to Olivia's house.

I don't know what's making me feel so future-positive this morning, but I have a feeling I have this damn Island and its constant cheeriness to thank for it. Or blame for it. Depending on how the day goes.

I use my hand to arrange the few wayward strands of hair back into place.

Flashes from my dream the night before filter into my mind. She never said yes. I remember the dream, which was more like a flashback of me proposing to Laura. And I don't know why it took me a solid seven months after the fact to realize it, but I realize it now. Laura never said yes.

She kissed me, she smiled, and we moved on forward from my proposal. We just kind of started planning the wedding.

She never said yes.

And isn't that a kicker? I scoff as I put on my sandals. Realize your ex-fiancée, who left you at the altar during your wedding, hadn't said the word 'Yes' to your proposal, seven months after the fact. Yeah, it's a kicker.

I pick up my phone from my nightstand. No messages from Alicia or Deaton. I walk to the front door, out of the house, and close the door behind me.

Where a few months ago, the knowledge of the kicker would have crushed me, and squeezed my heart in painful fists of hurt, now, as I walk past rows of flowers planted by the side of my driveway by God-knows-who, it doesn't seem to matter anymore.

I cover the short distance between my house and Olivia's. I press the doorbell, and a few seconds later, the door opens.

Olivia stands at the entrance, her short blonde hair waving slightly in the breeze of the morning. She is wearing a light pink top over a pair of jean shorts. I feel like I just drank a refreshing tall glass of water as I look at her.

She smiles as she sees me, and my heart lifts at the sight of it.

"Michael," she says my name in a whisper.

"Do you want to go on an unofficial date?" I ask.

Chapter 12

OLIVIA

9:25 a.m.

"Unofficial date." What the hell did that even mean?

He had explained, of course, when I had stood, staring at him like he had two heads. Or seven pairs of eyes.

He had said it was a date, but without the official rules of it.

Do I want to go on an unofficial date with Michael Rosenbaum, a hot single dad,- who just adds up hotness points by loving his daughter- doctor, sexy next-door neighbour, funny, and amazing man? Hmm. Yes.

Even with my cynical heart that is hella suspicious of happy-ever-afters, currently giving me a gazillion reasons why I should say no to the date... I said yes.

Now, he's in my living room, waiting for me, while I'm in my bedroom, freaking out.

I press a hand to my jittery stomach. Even though I have only had a bottle of water this morning, I feel like a circus is performing an act in my stomach. I press my head to my wardrobe door. Oh God, what have I done?

I want to talk to someone, a female, someone who can understand what I'm going through right now. I think of Alicia, but then I remember she was the one who had prepared the pink liquid stuff at the bonfire party, and I remember her crazy outfit that looked like it had been dipped in the rainbow. Alicia is probably not the sanest person to talk me down from this, I conclude.

My sister. She is the most practical, and probably the most grounded, person I know. But, we haven't talked in two years now. We didn't have a fight, no disagreement led to the years-long of silence, we had just drifted apart. She had gotten a job and had had to move to be closer to her workplace, and talking over the phone with a sister she had never really felt close to since our childhood years just didn't seem practical. To her, at least.

And slowly, one call a month became no calls at all. And that became two years later.

I shake my head to clear the nostalgic thoughts away. Now is not the time for a trip down memory lane. There is already enough traffic on the present-day lane, and the disastrous accident just waiting to happen, in my living room next door.

I close my eyes. "Okay, Jenkins, just calm the fuck down. This is not a big deal. This is not some 90's rom-com teenage movie. You are a grown-up adult woman, you have gone on dates before. Even though this is your first 'unofficial date'", I shake my head again to clear those thoughts away, "But that doesn't matter, because it is not a big deal."

I take a deep breath and open up the doors of my wardrobe. "Okay", I say with a release of breath.

Michael had said casual clothes. We were probably just going to take a stroll around the beach. Casual. I rifle through my wardrobe, on the hunt for casual (but not really) clothes.

10:20 a.m.

We walk side by side, purple ice cream cones in our hands. We actually just went to the beach. The breeze blows around my hair. People are scattered all around the beach. Some lie on chaise lounges and soak up the sun, and some run around, having fun.

I went with a cream-colored summery dress that cut off with a wavy hem at my knees. The gown hugs my frame and has a 'casual' feel to it. The subtle creamy tone of it knocks the dress out of the flashy category while blending perfectly with Michael's blue shirt. Finally, the flowery patterns on it just give it a happy look.

It was a winner as soon as I saw it.

I take a lick off my ice cream cone and look up at Michael. "So, unofficial date, huh? You use that a lot?"

He looks down at me, a small smile curving his lips. "No. It just seemed to apply here."

"Really? How?"

He shrugs lightly. "We are both single adults who find ourselves attracted to each other." He looks down at me as he says this. I swallow as I look into his eyes, but I don't say anything contrary. Michael breaks eye contact. We continue walking. "We both find being in each other's company pleasant. But we also both have issues we're dealing with. Emotionally", he adds, when I look up at him.

I don't say anything to that and after a moment of walking in silence, he says, "I see it in your eyes."

My heart trips a little at Michael's words. It's a little disconcerting to know he sees me so clearly. I don't know how to feel about that.

He shrugs, and his voice takes on a lighter tone. "So, an unofficial date seems perfect for us."

He smiles down at me, and after a brief hesitation, I smile back.

"So on this 'unofficial date'.... do we spill our guts? Let's lose the hurts that plague us from these emotional issues we both seem to have", I say, wriggling my eyebrows playfully.

"First off, don't you dare put 'air quotes' on our unofficial date? It's a real thing, Jenkins", he says, keeping his face as straight as possible. I hold back a laugh, as he continues, "Second, you don't have to spill anything you're not ready to." He pauses, and I see he is serious now as he says, "But I am. I'm ready to spill all my hurts," he looks down at me, "if you're ready to listen", he adds.

I look up at him, into his gray eyes. I nod.

He looks forward as we continue walking along the beach. His voice takes on a faraway tone.

"She was the most beautiful woman I had ever seen in my life....."

5:30 p.m.

We sit side by side, our legs lost in the sand. We are still at the beach. Our legs are bare, our sandals are sitting beside us as we sit in the sand.

Michael had talked about her for hours, the woman who had broken his heart. I frown as I realize now that he never really said her name. Huh.

I steal a glance at him. His hair is ruffled from the breeze, his face is relaxed, and there seems to be a stillness about it now. Not that he seemed restless before, but there's just a strange calmness in him now. Like he was finally free of some burden.

We hadn't only been talking about her since morning. We had veered off to other discussions around mid-afternoon. But now, as we sit in silence, the sun making its move to set, my mind goes back to her.

I wonder what the most beautiful woman to Michael would look like. Would she have long beautiful hair that reached down to her waist? My hand unconsciously goes to my short choppy hair. Would her eyes be really big and wide beautiful eyes? I know Michael isn't all about looks, but I bet she has one of those perfect hourglass figures, and her skin was a perfect blend of caramel brown.

I sigh silently. Who the hell looked like that? I just described a fucking cartoon mermaid character. I scoff at myself.

"What is it?" Michael asks me.

I look at him, at his handsome face, his clear green eyes that seems even clearer now, probably because of the ocean. Or his nearness. Our shoulders are almost touching, and like when I had looked into Julia's eyes for the first time, and it had felt like I was looking into eyes that I had known forever, I look into Michael's eyes now, and the same feeling runs through my head.

"What?" Michael asks again, now smiling.

I have been staring at him for a full minute.

I smile. "What did you love most about her?"

I hadn't meant to ask that. That wasn't the question I wanted to ask. I was going to ask something simple, like, her name. Why didn't I ask that?

I look at Michael's face, and I see he is surprised by the question too.

His brows furrow. "Oh, I- I don't know. I-" he looks at me again, and when I don't say anything, he looks back out at the ocean. His brows furrow even deeper as he thinks. His voice is quiet and deep when he says, "Sometimes, I loved everything about her, you know, she didn't even have to do anything, I just had to look at her." He pauses, and then he says, "While sometimes, the same things I loved about her, just made me sad."

Wow.

We both look at the ocean as the waves lap over each other. The sound of it is the only thing between us, as we both stare at it silently.

And I realize I am afraid to ask Michael what he likes about me. I'm afraid to hear the answer.

"So, on this unofficial date, do we kiss at the end of it?" I ask instead, looking up at him with a smile, so he knows I'm teasing.

He looks down at me, he smiles back. "We'll see."

Chapter 13

MICHAEL

Tuesday. 2:30 p.m.

I look around the hall, not even trying to hide the fact that I'm looking anymore. They all already think we are dating anyway, so what's the damage?

It's been three days since I took Olivia out on an unofficial date. I still give myself kudos for coming up with that on the fly. I hadn't thought about it until I was standing on her doorstep. And it had worked out well too. We had walked by the beach, which to me was the perfect spot for an unconventional date like mine and Olivia's unofficial date. The gentle breeze, the sounds of the ocean's waves overlapping, people lounging, relaxing, and having fun. We had talked, which I can now admit had been the main purpose of my asking Olivia out on the date.

After having that dream/flashback of the time I proposed to Laura, the need to let go of that period of my life, my time with Laura, materialized. I knew talking about it, especially to a woman I think I could come to really care about, was the first step. And, she had listened.

I run a hand nervously through my hair. Had I talked about Laura too much? I didn't know it when I was talking about her, but maybe I had talked about her a little too much. And talking about my ex for too long is probably a big red flag to a woman I potentially want to date, right? I hear the question replay in my head. Oh... It is.

I close my eyes. Crap. I open them again. I pace back and forth a little. I run my hand through my hair again. Where is she?

It's been three days since our date, and I haven't seen Olivia since. The day after our date, Friday, I received an email from Alicia, it had listed out my responsibilities for the carnival party. I had been mildly surprised at the formality of it all. Alicia and Deaton were not especially known for their sense of formality. She had written in the email that we, the carnival party planning committee, were to meet the next day, Saturday, in the hall, to discuss whatever we didn't quite understand, or didn't like, in the email. Seeing as she had put me in charge of music and lighting, I had predicted I would have a lot to disagree with. But mostly, I had been excited to see Olivia again.

She hadn't come. All through the meeting, I had kept waiting for her to come through the doors, but she hadn't. I had gone on to inform Alicia of my belief in my inability to deliver the kind of music people would love at a carnival. She hadn't believed me, so I had shown her my Spotify playlists. She had taken one look at my oldies artists, and she had promised to find another thing for me to do for the carnival.

I had gone home after the meeting, and eventually walked over to Olivia's house, to ask why she hadn't shown up for the meeting. Her lights had been off, and I had rung the bell several times and got no response.

I hadn't seen her all through Sunday too. She hadn't been at home either. I know, cause I had watched her house almost all day.

And then yesterday, we had another carnival party planning committee- I'm just going to start calling it CPPC- meeting. Olivia hadn't shown up for that either.

Today is Tuesday, we have another CCPC meeting. I am in the hall where we have the meetings, and still no sign of Olivia. I'm starting to get worried now.

Just then, Alicia walks past me, there is an ear pod in her ear and she's carrying a notepad. She looks busy.

I jog to catch up with her. "Hey, Alicia."

She turns to me. "Michael. Did you see my email? I put you in charge of hiring the clown. For the kids."

Alicia hadn't stopped walking, so now I'm walking alongside her. "I know zero about clown, Alicia, zero."

She waves that off like it's unimportant. "Nobody knows clown parties, Michael. Just find one, and hire them."

"I'm going to botch it, Alicia," I say, looking down at her pointedly.

She looks up at me, and then sighs. "Fine. You're off clown duty." She looks down at the notepad on her clipboard. "The only thing left here is cups. Oh, and ice," she looks up at me, and smiles, "You're in charge of cups and ice."

Cups and ice. Uh. I suddenly feel like Phoebe during Rachel's birthday in an episode of Friends. But I think about it, and I don't see a way I could botch up cups and ice. And if worse comes to worst, I'll have a TV show episode to guide me.

"Great," I say. "Hey, have you heard from Olivia by any chance? She hasn't been coming to meetings, and I'm starting to get worried."

Alicia gives me a distracted look, before looking back down at her clipboard. She ticks things off. "Oh, she's fine. She called me on Friday, asking if she could work from home since she didn't need to be at the meetings for her side of things."

"Oh."

"Yeah. She's been at home all this while. Why, I went over to her place just yesterday."

She had been at home all this while? Why was she acting like she wasn't? Was she avoiding me?

I frown, that thought doesn't sit well with me.

"Oh, but she says she's coming in today though. She says she has some samples of cakes for us to taste," Alicia says. She continues walking on, I stop following her.

Olivia is coming to the hall today. That's good. We can finally talk, and I can figure out if she was avoiding me all this while.

We hadn't kissed. After our unofficial date on Thursday, we hadn't kissed.

We had both walked to our houses later in the night after our talk by the beach. She had looked up at me, and smiled that smile of hers. The one that lights up her face, and makes my breath catch in my throat.

I had looked down at her, and I had thought about kissing her. Hell, it had been the only thought in my head. And the beat of my heart as it pounded had been the only sound roaring in my ears. But somehow, I hadn't kissed her. It had been like something was stopping me from closing the distance between our lips.

I had looked down at her, she up at me, and something had stopped me from closing the distance between us.

I look up, the hair on my neck stands up, and I see her. She stands at the entrance of the hall, carrying a box. She is wearing a simple light pink top over a pair of blue jeans, and she looks the same as she had three days ago, and yet somehow, she looks different.

She looks around the room, searching for something. Someone. Her eyes lock on mine. I see her eyes twitch slightly. She grips the box tightly.

I walk over to her and stop in front of her.

"I didn't kiss you," I say.

Her eyelids dilate a bit at my words, but then they go blank. She looks away. I bring her face back to mine, so she's looking directly at me. I know the enormity of this moment.

"I didn't kiss you. And because it isn't just about me not kissing you, you have been avoiding me. Me not kissing you meant something was stopping me. It meant something was standing between us."

Olivia looks up at me. "What was standing between us, Michael?"

I hadn't figured it out until I saw her walk into the hall a few seconds ago.

"Laura," I say.

Olivia's eyes narrow slightly, and I realize this is the first time I'm saying Laura's name out loud to Olivia.

Well, I'm breaking barriers now. I'm breaking down that wall that was standing between us the night of our unofficial date. The night I should have kissed Olivia.

"Laura was standing between us, her memories, the love I felt for her, everything that she was. Talking about her brought her to our middle. Recounting who she was and what we were to each other, brought her alive."

Olivia doesn't say anything, she just keeps looking up at me. None of what she must be feeling as I talk, yet again, about my ex, shows on her face. And I can't read her.

But, I'm breaking down walls.

"I had a dream about her the night before, to the morning of, our date." I see Olivia swallow. "And I wanted to finally let her go because I could finally admit to myself that I had been holding on to her still." I cup Olivia's face with my hands and look into her eyes. "And I did. I let her go."

There are no walls now.

I lean in and gently close the distance between our lips.

Chapter 14

OLIVIA

3:00 p.m.

I close my eyes as Michael's lips meet mine. Feelings run through me, emotions swirl around in my head. A zing runs up my spine, my toes curl and my head swims.

Finally. The thought runs through my head. *Finally.*

Ever since that night, the night when Michael didn't kiss me, I have been thinking. A lot. First, I have been thinking about why he didn't kiss me. Why? And then, I have been thinking about what it meant, him not kissing me. I have been thinking about what it meant for us that he didn't kiss me.

But mostly, I have been thinking about him kissing me. I have been thinking about that a lot.

And now, he is finally kissing me.

I get lost in it. Michael's lips are warm and moist on mine, and I feel myself shudder as he continues kissing me still.

I am aware in a very far and distant part of my mind, that I am carrying a box with cakes inside. And I am also aware, in that same distant part of my mind, that we are standing in a hall full of people, and that they were probably right now standing and watching us.

But I don't acknowledge any of these things. I am aware of them, but I don't acknowledge them. Because the roaring in my head is all I hear, and the feel of Michael's lips on mine is all I acknowledge.

Finally, he lets me go.

He looks down at me, and I up at him. I look into his eyes, and I see how clear they are. They are clouded with desire because he just finished rocking my world with that kiss, but beneath the clouds, I see the clearness.

He really has let go of Laura. He is looking only at me now, thinking only of me. He is very focused on me.

My chest constricts. Licks of panic filter around my heart. This strong, amazing man, who had his heart broken by a woman he loved fiercely with all his heart, has cleared out his heart. For me.

I know now, even as I look up into his eyes, and he into mine, I know he is offering it to me. He is offering his heart to me.

And my chest constricts again. The licks of panic turn into full-blown panic.

"I have to go," I mutter.

Before Michael can say another word, I hastily walk away.

Strangely, my eyes start to water, and the water blurs my vision as I walk. I keep my head down as I pass people by. Even then, I can feel eyes on me.

EMMA LENA

I see a door just a few feet in front of me. I walk towards it and push the door open. I try to adjust my eyes to the interior of the small room, and after a few seconds, I see it's a room of some sort.

I place the box I'm carrying gently on one of the stools I see there, and I drop to the floor.

I cover my face with my hands and start sobbing.

I don't even know why I'm crying. Even as I continue to cry, I don't know why.

Maybe it's because I recognize the squeeze on my heart as my default sign for when I'm starting to self-sabotage when I meet a really good guy. Michael is a really good guy. After Ethan, I was almost certain I would never meet a guy as good as him again. But of course, I meet Michael. Michael is even better! What is this curse?

I lift my head to look up at the ceiling of the room. How could I meet someone even better than Ethan? And now, I'm left feeling even more conflicted than I felt with Ethan.

It would have been better if Michael couldn't get over her because then I would have a reason not to fall in love with him. But, now, he's over her, and he's looking at me. Me.

Laura. Why Laura?

I think of my sister. Her name is Laura too.

Why did the name of Michael's love have to be Laura?

I wipe the tears away from my face. Isn't that just screwy? The fact that the man I am starting to like, once loved, like truly loved, a woman with the same name as my estranged sister. Yeah, that is screwy.

The squeeze on my heart is starting to relieve me. I don't feel the urge to cry anymore. I stand up from the floor and dust off my legs.

I just left Michael out there. God, I'm a terrible person. The man rocked my world with a kiss, and I just left him out there. Amid those gossip-hungry wolves.

Michael's green eyes flash through my mind again. He is over her. I could see that clearly in his eyes. He has moved on from her. But does moving on from someone mean that person would never love another like he loved the one he moved on from?

I lift the box from the stool. Could Michael ever love like he loved Laura, ever again?

I walk out of the room with this disturbing thought on my mind.

4:00 p.m.

Alicia and two other women sit behind the wide table. One of the women's names, as Alicia introduced us earlier on, is Whitney. She is a bleached blonde woman with a nice smile and a gentle personality. The other woman, also a nice woman, but with black hair and piercing green eyes, her name is Dana. She is Alicia's friend and go-to baker. She owns a bakery in Catalina Island and is famously known for making tasty baked goodies.

I had looked at her uncomfortably when Alicia had introduced me as the baker for the carnival party. But she had just laughed and told me not to worry about any thoughts I might have on infringing on her turf. Dana and her husband were both moving away to Paris, tomorrow.

I nodded in relief and understanding. If anyone was going to move away from Catalina Island, the person could only be moving to somewhere even more beautiful, like Paris.

I have come to love Catalina so much. The people, and the ambiance of the Island itself. Its calming and soothing presence. I had come here to escape, and I had found a haven. I realize how dependent I have become on the island. The only thing marring my stay is this conflicting thought over Michael.

After leaving the store/closet, I had gone in search of Alicia. I had brought samples of the deserts I had baked for the carnival, and I wanted her to taste them and give me the go-ahead. Or not.

The box is open in front of the three women, on the wide table. Alicia's eyes are closed as she savours the lemon meringue cupcake she is currently holding. Whitney had taken the blueberry muffin, and Dana had taken the carrot cupcake.

I wait as they each take bites from their cakes, and I realize I am kind of nervous about their opinions. I am a certified baker, with up to ten years of experience in baking under my belt, and a bakery back home. Yet, I find myself nervous about what three random women thought about my cakes.

Whitney looks at me, smiling. "This is the best blueberry muffin I have ever tasted."

Again, I look at Dana. She just smiles at me. "Hey, don't look at me. This is the best carrot cake I have ever eaten."

I smile. "Thank you," I say to both of them. I turn to Alicia.

Alicia smiles. "You already know what I'm going to say." She looks at both women on each side of her, and then back at me. "Please bake your cakes for the carnival party."

Whitney and Dana laugh. I smile. "I'd be honored."

The three women stand up, signalling the end of the tasting round. I stand up too. As we walk towards the door, Dana turns to me.

"Hey, I'm looking to sell my bakery. Are you interested? I'm sure everybody would be delighted to have a new baker in town once I'm gone."

"Oh, I'm not, well, I'm not planning on staying here permanently."

Dana blinks. "Oh. I didn't know." She smiles, "Well, if you change your mind, Alicia has my number, you can just call me, and we'll talk prices."

Dana walks away, I wave at her back.

Catalina Island's baker. A bakery that is already well known by Catalina Island's residents. A choice to live, and work, in Catalina. New friends, new opportunities, new life. Michael.

Oh, so much to gain. So very much to gain.

Chapter 15

MICHAEL

Four months ago.

Michael and Laura's wedding day.

This is it. This is the day I finally tie myself to the woman of my dreams.

And I'm not just getting a wife today, I'm getting a complete family. Just two weeks ago, our little bundle of joy, Julia, had come into the world.

She had come a little earlier- apparently, my baby girl is impatient- but, thankfully, I had been off duty that day, and we had been able to get to the hospital with no hiccups. She also had a flair for the dramatic, because when we got to the hospital, there had been no empty delivery rooms. Everyone had been occupied, with either birth-in-progress or nearly-there. A makeshift delivery room had to be created just for Julia.

But, 45 minutes later- like I said, impatient- Julia came into the world screaming her lungs out.

Maybe she'd become a singer. That octave had been loud! I grin to myself as I remember it. I already had plans for her, and she could be anything she wanted to be. I can already see my baby girl will be a force to be reckoned with.

I shift on my feet as I look out at the guests seated. I see family. My parents, cousins, aunts, uncles, nieces, nephews, and even our family dog, Cassie, is here. They are all smiling and waiting for my bride. I am glad they're here. We don't talk as often as we should, but we have always pulled through on important days such as this one. My friends, a couple from college, more from work, and all my neighbours throughout my block, are all here.

Laura hadn't invited a lot of people. A few people from her workplace, Innocence, which I had invited myself. Laura hadn't wanted to invite anybody at all.

She hardly talks about her family, but I know her dad is no longer in the picture, but her mom and sister were. Though she hardly ever talks to them either anymore. I had tried to pry information out of her, but Laura can be pretty determined when she sets her mind to something. That was one of the things I love about her.

But sadly, she doesn't have anyone in the way of family to be here for her today. I had invited her work friends because even though I could just investigate her family behind her back, and invite them over, I know Laura would probably hate me for it. Her work colleagues were the safer choice.

I adjust my tie again; the sun is vicious today. Even under the canopy, I'm standing with Levy and the minister, the sun still manages to penetrate its warmth.

Suddenly, people start murmuring, and I see some of the guests shifting restlessly in their seats.

I frown and turn to Levy. "What are they murmuring about?"

Levy looks at me with a.... sad.... look? What is going on?

"Um-" whatever Levy was going to say gets cut off as our attention both get drawn to the end of the aisle. Everybody else's attention gets drawn there too.

Laura's maid of honor, Gabriella, stands at the end of the aisle. She is a woman of small stature and is the total opposite of Laura when it comes to looks. Where Laura's hair is black, hers is a flaming red, where Laura's face confidently says bold, hers whispers shy. She had taken on the position of Laura's maid of honor just this morning when I explained to her that Laura didn't have a maid of honor. Her hazel eyes- another contrast to Laura's blue ones- had gone wide at the thought of a bride not having a maid of honor. She had wrung her small hands and bit the corner of her lips, both obvious signs of nervousness, as she had said she wasn't sure she and Laura were close enough for her to be her maid of honor. I had told her not to worry about that, and to just help out her friend, no matter how casual a friend she was to her.

The same small hands are now gripping the small bouquet in her hands, tightly. Her eyes dart to chairs where the guests are seated, and staring back at her, wide-eyed, back to me. And then, they fill up with tears.

"Why is she- why is she crying? Where's Laura?" I ask no one in particular, but Levy lays a hand on my shoulder. I look over at him. "What- why are you-" I trail off.

I know what is happening right now. I'm not a fool. Or, maybe I am, since it's happening to me. But I don't want to believe it's happening to me.

I look at my parents, their wise eyes that seem to already know what is happening too, and they look back at me. My mom starts to make her way toward me, my dad puts a hand on her arm to stop her. Good, I think to myself, I don't think I want anyone near me right now.

I glance at the minister, who is looking at me with the same eyes my parents were looking at me. Eyes that knew what was going on. I look at the remaining guests, and I see mixtures of pity and shock on their faces.

I walk down the aisle, towards Gabriella who is still standing at the end of the aisle, gripping the flowers in her hand. I don't look at her as I walk past her. I already know what's in her eyes. I already know this is the worst day of my life.

Present day. Wednesday. 9:15 a.m.

I turn off my car's engine and just throw my head back on my car seat. I close my eyes, and rub at the tension on my forehead, between my eyes.

I had had another dream about Laura. Last night's dream had been particularly vicious. Our wedding day. The day Laura had broken my heart. I hadn't seen it. Later, much later, after the day Laura didn't show up to her wedding, I got the vibe from Levy that he kind of suspected Laura would not turn up. But I hadn't seen it. I hadn't even gotten a smidge, talk less of suspicion, from Laura.

I had thought that day was the worst day of my life, but it wasn't. The worst day of my life came a day later, when I opened my door, and found Julia in a basket, with a note from Laura.

Nope, not going there. I open my eyes and lift my head from my car seat. I shake it lightly as if to erase the memory from my head.

Why did she leave the way she did? The memory of Olivia running- okay, walking very fast- away from me, after I kissed her yesterday, burn into my brain. Why had she run away?

What is it with women running away from me when I want to make some kind of commitment to them?

I guess if I was a shrink, I would say the similarities between Olivia running away from me yesterday and Laura not showing up on our wedding day, are very monumental. And maybe, just maybe, that was the reason for the dream materializing last night.

I sigh. I can't sit in this funk anymore. I look back at Julia in her car seat. Her eyes are open, and on me as she stares at me.

"Okay, Doc, we're going in."

I open the door and get out of my car. I release the car seat buckle and carry Julia as I walk toward the hall.

We have another CPPC meeting today, and Olivia will be around. I confirmed with Alicia. We are going to talk about what happened between us yesterday, like adults, and I'm going to get answers. This fucking shit hurts too much for a second time around.

I push open the doors to the hall and walk in. My eyes search the crowd of people already there, no sign of Olivia. My eyes track over to a corner of the hall, where a giant monstrosity of a machine stands.

I frown. *What the hell is that?* The machine is a big piece of equipment, with sharp earth-like structures surrounding the edges of it. The sharp structures are like an attachment to the whole of the machine, and they are laid down on the floor.

Someone could get really hurt on that, I think to myself. I look around the room, trying to find Alicia or Deaton, and let them know. I see Alex and his friend, a boy I recognize from Alex's birthday, Is- something, Isaiah? Israel? They run around the hall, chasing each other in what looks to be a passionate game of cops and robbers. Well, cop and robber, in their case.

I take my eyes off of them for a second, to look around, once again, for Alicia or Deaton. And that one second was all it took.

I hear a piercing scream from the other side of the room.

Chapter 16

OLIVIA

9:25 a.m.

It sounded like an agonizing cry of a wolf who just lost her baby. But filled with even more pain.

My head swivels towards the sound of the shrill cry that just pierced through the hall. My eyes sharpen on the far end of the hall where the ugly machine I had seen as I walked into the hall earlier on, was. A few groups of people have gathered around the spot, and I can hear murmurs from them, I see the panicked expressions on their faces. I walk towards it, like every other person in the hall.

Alicia passes by me in a run, and I see that Deaton is already at the scene of the commotion. He is on his knees, as I see through the small space between the legs of people standing. They are gathered around who had probably let out that scream.

I get to the group and try to see over their shoulders what was causing the commotion. I hear murmurs of 'Oh God', and I hear someone say 'Oh, that is just too much blood.' That is when I see the blood on the floor.

I push my way through the bodies of the crowd until I finally see the scene in front of me. Alicia is now on her knees too, next to Deaton. They are bent over a small boy, I look at his face and recognize him as Alex's friend from his birthday party, Isaac. I remember his name. When he introduced himself to me, he said how he thought his name was cool because his namesake in the bible had been almost sacrificed before God had stopped it. He had been so cute I had just nodded and smiled at him.

I look at him now, at his young face twisted in pain as he cried openly like a baby. Something I'm sure he would never have done if he wasn't in so much pain.

My eyes trail down to his leg, where blood is currently gushing out in spurts of bright red.

"Oh God," I mutter with the others standing near Isaac.

The third person crouched down next to Isaac, looks up at the sound of my voice. My eyes meet his, and I see that it's Michael. Even with the horrific situation in front of me, my pulse kicks up a notch as Michael's green eyes bore into mine.

I haven't seen him since the kiss yesterday when I had left him standing in this very same hall. My cheeks turn flush. Michael's gaze leaves mine and returns to Isaac. Mine does too.

A woman is crouched down next to Isaac's head. She is bawling all over him as she says his name over and over again. Alicia tries to pry her away from Isaac.

"Come on now, Anna, you know you must not jostle him," Alicia tries to get the woman away from Isaac gently by lifting her arms.

The woman, who has a similar color of hair to Isaac's, I assume is his mother, continues crying even as she lets herself be lifted away from Isaac. I look over at Alex, he stands a few feet away from the scene, looking close to tears. His eyes are filled with them already, his hands are on Julia's stroller in front of him, and from where I'm standing, I can only see a part of Julia's face.

I see Michael look over to Alex and Julia, and then he looks back down at Isaac. I can see he is struggling to divide his attention equally between them. I walk over to where Alex is and put a hand over his shoulders. I put my hand on Julia's stroller too, beside Alex's hand.

Michael looks at me, gratitude in his eyes, just before he looks back down at Isaac.

"Do you think it's broken?" Deaton directs the question to Michael.

Michael looks down at Isaac's leg, it was twisted into a position that even I could tell wasn't a normal position. But I see Michael look at Isaac's mom, he looks at Alicia, and a look passes between them. The same look passes between Alicia and Deaton.

"I can't fully ascertain that from here, I need to take a scan and some tests to be sure," Michael says.

He looks at Alicia again, giving her a signal. She nods slightly and whispers to Isaac's mom. After a lot of tugging and whispering, the woman finally allows herself to be pulled away from Isaac. Alicia guides her away from the scene, a few women that had gathered, follow Alicia, consoling Isaac's mom.

As they leave, Michael turns to Deaton. "We need an ambulance, he needs to go to the hospital for a scan asap."

Deaton nods. "Yeah, I know. I have to go to the hospital though, to get a better response time. The ambulance is probably dispatched to another place right now as we speak. We get a lot of emergencies, mostly from vacationers taking a hike or some other sporting event."

Michael looks down at Isaac's leg again, and then back up at Deaton. "Okay, okay, sure, go. I'll try to hold down the fort here," he says.

Deaton nods and stands up to leave. He puts a hand on Michael's shoulder, "I'm glad you're here, man," he says. He leaves, jogging towards the entrance of the hall. One of the bystanders offers to drive him.

I look at Michael as he looks at Isaac. He smiles at him, even as the boy looks on at him with terrified eyes.

"Isaac, right?" Michael asks. Isaac nods a little, his tears reduced to sniffling now. "Okay, Isaac, we're going to wait for Uncle Deaton to get back with the ambulance. In the meantime, you have to be strong for me, okay, buddy?"

"There's a lot of blood," Isaac says, his breath hitching as he looks down at his leg, his cheeks are stained with dried tears.

"I know, I know, buddy, but don't worry about it, okay? I don't want you to worry about it, because we're going to fix you up well. Uncle Deaton and I. Okay?"

Michael keeps his eyes steady on Isaac's until he nods.

I turn to Alex. "Stay here with Julia, okay? Stay here with her." I wait until Alex nods his head in the affirmative before I walk to where Michael is.

I kneel beside Michael, looking down at Isaac with him. The people that previously formed had thinned out some, with most of the women had followed Alicia and Isaac's mom.

"I need to make a makeshift tourniquet, to stop the bleeding. I can't do anything about the leg until I get to the hospital, but I need to stop the bleeding," Michael says.

"What do you need?" I ask him, eager to help.

He looks at me, and a look passes in his eyes, but he doesn't say anything. He just nods and starts listing things I'll need to get.

When he's done, I get to my feet, and walk to the supply closet I had closed myself in the day before after Michael had kissed me. God, that seemed like a month ago now. Some of the men that had been standing around the scene of the accident followed me. We grabbed the things Michael had asked me to get and walk back to where Isaac and Michael are. We lay them down on the floor, and Michael starts working on him.

I look at Isaac, his young terrified eyes scream with pain. I smile easily at him. "Hey, Isaac, remember me? I was at your best friend's birthday party. Alex's birthday party." He just looks at me with blank eyes. Blank maybe from shock, or just ignorance, I couldn't tell. But I just continue talking anyway. "You told me you liked your name, that it was cool cause of the bible reference," I see a spark of recognition in his eyes as I say this. I smile again. "Yeah, you remember." I take his hand in mine, and he grips it, hard. "I'm here, your mom is here, and Michael?" "He's a doctor, an orthopaedic surgeon." That means his job is mainly to fix bones. That's all he ever does. And he's good at it too. You're in safe hands, Isaac. Trust me."

I maintain eye contact with him, and when I'm sure he believes every word I said, I turn to Michael.

I work with him as he applies the tourniquet, holding on to whatever he needs me to hold on to, lifting whatever needs to be lifted. We work slowly, and carefully, side by side until the tourniquet is successfully put in place.

I look down at Isaac's leg, and I can already see the blood reduced. Alicia and Isaac's mom come back and she kneels beside his head and holds his hand. The sound of the ambulance arriving outside brings all our heads up. Michael looks over at Julia's stroller.

My eyes follow his. I put a hand on his arm. "I've got her."

Chapter 17

MICHAEL

8:30 p.m.

I drag my feet as I make my way to Olivia's house.

Climbing the steps up to Olivia's doorstep, I run a hand over the back of my neck. I feel fatigue deep in every part of my body and in my eyes. My body screams sore muscles.

I press the bell and wait for her to answer. A few seconds later, I hear Olivia's feet walking to the door. She opens the door and her blonde hair, curled up in a messy bun on the top of her head, with her faded tee and messy cut-off jeans, all present a view that made something in my exhausted body sigh.

Her eyes shine with clear concern as she looks at me.

"Hey," she says, and steps aside to let me in.

I muster up a small smile as I enter. "Hey."

"You must be so exhausted," she says.

"All in a day's work," my tone coming out dry. "I hope Julia didn't give you too much trouble."

She waves my comment off. "Oh please, that baby girl of yours is as sweet as they come, and you know it. She was an angel. I was so glad to hear that Isaac is doing okay now. It must have been crazy, having to do an emergency surgery that you hadn't planned for."

I sigh and rested against her kitchen countertop. I run a hand through my hair. "It was. I kind of suspected before we drove to the hospital, that it was bad. Like, bad enough to maybe need surgery." I shake my head, "I didn't even think about the fact that I would be the one to do it. I completely forgot that CIMC didn't have an orthopaedic surgeon on their roster."

Olivia frowned. "But if they don't have an orthopaedic surgeon, doesn't that mean they wouldn't have the tools you needed too?"

I blow out a breath. "I was surprised too, but they had everything on standby, and more to the point, in place, by the time we arrived there. I hadn't even been sure he was going to need surgery until I did the scans. But they had had it all laid out just in case."

"Come on," Olivia says and leads me to a stool in the kitchen. She points to it, indicating I should sit.

I hesitate for just a second, before taking my seat. Even with all the craziness of today's drama, I haven't forgotten how things are between us.

She walks to her fridge and brings out a pitcher of water. She reaches for a glass cup from a cupboard above her head. She stands on her toes, trying to complement the difference in her height to the cupboard. Her creamy legs stretch out in all their glory, courtesy of the shorts, and her tee stretch over her upper body. My aching body tightens even more.

Taking my eyes off Olivia's tempting body, I do myself a favor and look down at the counter.

She walks over to the counter, and puts down the cup; she pours water into it and slides it across the counter to me.

I take a drink, glancing at her appreciatively.

She smiles. "Isa, Isaac's mom, I'm sure she must have been so grateful to you," Olivia says. She's looking at me like I'm some superhero.

I shrug, feeling a tad uncomfortable. "Yeah, she was. I was just doing my job though."

"Maybe, but that doesn't mean she wouldn't still be grateful. You didn't just save her son's life, you helped him so that he can continue to run with his best friend, even after this."

I shrug again, because, really, what am I supposed to say to that?

"I was just doing my job. And what about you? Taking on a scared thirteen-year-old boy and a baby, all on your own, just out of the blue like that," steering the conversation, and praise, from me to Olivia.

She smiles. "It was nothing. You had to go, and someone had to look after Alex and Julia. I was the someone."

"Now who's being modest? I know people who would have balked at the idea of having a baby on their hands without prior plans, and having to be responsible for a baby and a teenage boy all day."

Now, it was her turn to shrug. "Julia makes it easy, and Alex was mostly just scared for his best friend. All I had to do was assure him that Isaac was going to be fine. Like a hundred times. No biggie." She chuckles softly. I smile back. "But it was tough on him. He cares about Isaac."

"Yeah, I could see that." "We wrapped up the surgery around mid-afternoon, but I had to stay back to monitor his vitals and stuff. He had a rough going of it for a while, in the afternoon, but he pulled through. He's a tough kid."

Olivia smiles. "I'm glad. Alicia was calling during the day to update me. I guess she knew I would likely go crazy if I didn't get updates," she smiles wryly. "She says Deaton assisted."

I nod, taking another sip of water. "Yeah. He didn't have to, and he's way overqualified for it, but he just wanted to help, I guess. Lots of the hero stuff going around, huh?"

Olivia smiles, the smile lights up her face and my heart thumps wildly in my chest. God, she's beautiful, I think to myself.

My mind flashes back to yesterday, when I had kissed her, and she had left me standing in the hall. My chest squeezes painfully, and I look down at the almost-empty glass of water. What am I doing here? She didn't reciprocate when I kissed her, so what the hell am I doing here?

I remember the hurt I had experienced when the consequences of Laura not showing up at the altar had finally sunk in. The heartbreak I had felt knowing Laura hadn't planned on saying her vows to me as I had planned on saying mine to her. The pain of realizing that I had been the only one ready to start the rest of our lives. And how even more crushing that pain had been when I realized it had probably been only me with the feelings all the while we were together. The thought that our love had been one-sided.

Now, when I think about the whole thing, I think that more than anything, what was grated about the whole wedding affair. The fact that while I had been busy being happy about finding out Laura was pregnant and making plans for the future, Laura had doubts all along. I hadn't seen them then, and she hadn't said a word. Damn it, she should have said something.

Maybe she hadn't said anything because she had been afraid, I would have not let her go so easily. And yes, I admit I wouldn't have just let her go like that. I was in love. I would have fought for the woman I love, even if I was fighting against the woman herself.

But, at the end of it all, after trying everything I can to make her stay, I would have let her go. If she wanted to go still, I would have let her go. So why didn't she say something? Why did she let me build my hopes and dreams on something that was not going anywhere? That grates. That singular fact, grates.

I'd be damned if I do it all a second time.

I push myself up off the stool and look at Olivia. "I better go. Where's Julia?"

The silence hangs between us. I'm laying it all out on the table now. It's all or nothing. Either I stay, and we see where this goes, or I leave, and the moment I do, it's over. I look into her eyes, and I see she knows. She knows this is the turning point, so I leave the decision to her.

I watch her eyes stare back at me, boring into mine. She lets all she's thinking flash nakedly across her face. I see fear, insecurity, and nerves, all at war with the desire to grab what she wants, which is standing right in front of her, me. I let her see everything on my face too. I lay my soul bare and as nakedly vulnerable to her as I can.

This is all I can do. This is all I will do.

After another tense moment, Olivia swallows visibly, and says in a small voice, "Why don't you stay? I have a bottle of wine I have been meaning to open up for a while now."

I look at her, she smiles tentatively. I smile back, slowly. "I'd love that."

Chapter 18

OLIVIA

Thursday. 8:05 a.m.

I open my eyes slowly, feeling the early morning sun's warmth on my face. My hand naturally goes out to the other side of my bed.

My eyes open as I hear an 'ow' come from the other side of the bed. Michael. I look sideways at him, there is a light irritated scowl on his face. I look back up at the ceiling.

Michael, in my house. In my room. On my bed. I close my eyes as the memories from last night flash through my mind. The very tense minutes when Michael had given me an ultimatum: stay, or go. That very life-changing moment I had chosen 'stay'.

The moments afterward. Michael checking on Julia. Coming back to the living room, each of us having a glass of wine, sitting on the couch, and talking about ourselves. Our family. I had left out my sister for some reason I still don't understand, even now. I guess the same-name thing with his ex is just too creepy for me.

And when we had been all talked out, (or, what I think really happened; when we had not been able to ignore the sexual tension that had been brimming between us as we had talked, anymore) we jumped each other.

That is the honest-to-God accurate description. We jumped at each other. I don't know who lunged first, but lips and hands met, and it was a frenzy of releasing the built-up tension.

After kissing for what had seemed like an eternity last night on the couch, Michael had carried me into the room. I had had the best night of my life. Our one-night stand on the beach comes in second now.

I look over at Michael now, the sun streams in through the window, and slants over his face, softening his features.

Where there had been a scowl before, there was now a huge grin on his face.

"Morning, Jenkins. You asked me to stay," he says. He is on his side, his head pillowed on his hands. He smiles at me, a cat-like kind of grin, and I just can't help it. I smile back.

I mirror his position. "I did?" I ask rhetorically.

"So, regrets?" Michael asks. He asks the question lightly, and I see the teasing glint in his eyes, but I also see the doubts. He is nervous. This beautifully amazing man is nervous I might not want him anymore.

My throat closes up as I stare at him. His black full hair, his eyebrows as they arch over his eyes, those green eyes that had gotten to me from the very first moment they looked at me, into me. His nose, his defined cheekbones, his mouth. The lips that had ravaged me just a few hours ago, lips that had left trails of emotions in their wake as they trailed all over my body. Lips that had taken me to heights of pleasure I hadn't even known existed before last night.

"No regrets," I whisper, looking directly into Michael's eyes.

He looks right back into mine, and a thousand words pass between us without either of us uttering a word. Michael brings his fingers up between us and opens them wide. I look at them, frowning, wondering what he is doing. He clocks his head slightly at them and looks at my hand. I lift my hand and intertwine my fingers with his.

I look at him, he looks at me. He smiles, and automatically, I just smile too. The sun streams down on his face, and my breath catches.

I think I am seeing the most beautiful image I have ever seen in my life.

And then he grins again. "What is for breakfast around here?"

He kisses me on my forehead, gets up from the bed, buck naked, and walks to the edge of the bedpost. He puts on his trousers, turns to me, winks, and strolls out of the room.

I watch his sexy back as he walks out. I grin, and fall back on the bed. God, I love him!

I open my eyes as the feeling settles in me. With the warm feel of the sun on my skin, I feel the emotion go through my whole body.

I love Michael.

I smile again. I am in love. And it is such a wholesome feeling that I do not even feel the squeeze on my heart that reminds me of the fear of commitment I usually have. I feel like committing. Hell, I am committed.

I jump out of the bed- much like Michael did- with a burst of energy, and skip to the kitchen. Yeah, I skip.

I enter the kitchen and see Michael already standing behind the counter, drinking a glass of water. He smiles at me, I smile back.

I'm walking towards him when my phone on the counter rings. I glance at it, and I almost want to ignore it. I am too damn happy for the world to intrude right now. But I pick it up anyway.

"Hello?" I don't recognize the number, I frown as a strange voice asks me if I am Olivia Jenkins. "This is she," curious. The strange voice asks me if I'm a sister to one Laura Jenkins. Concerned now, I answer, "Yes, I am."

And then the strange voice goes on to shatter my new, shiny, bright, love-filled world, by telling me my sister, a person I hadn't talked to in two years because of something I don't even remember, was in a fatal accident. He tells me to come right away because there might not be much time left.

The phone falls from my hand, and I instantly feel Michael beside me. He is asking me what's wrong, but his voice sounds like it's coming from a faraway place.

I turn to him, I use the sound of his voice as a guide out of the dark tunnel I suddenly find myself in. I hold on to him, he's like an anchor to me right now. He holds on right back.

"My sister. She was in an accident. They said there's probably not much time left. I have to go," I say blankly, unable to feel the raw emotion that was welling up in my eyes.

"We have to go," Michael says.

I look blankly at him. "But-"

He cuts me off. "I'll drive. Let me get my keys and Julia. Stay right here, okay?"

He leaves me standing in the middle of my suddenly too-bright kitchen.

He didn't even know where we are going. My eyes fill up with tears.

I stand and wait for Michael to come back, and take care of everything.

8:30 p.m.

We pull up in front of my house. A house that now looks even bigger because of the heaviness of my heart.

My sister of.... the years of my whole life.... who I had ignored for the past two years, died today.

And I got the call because she had put me on as her emergency contact. Not because they had found my number on her recent calls.

I rub a hand over my chest. It has been hurting like hell ever since the shattering call this morning, and I have been rubbing on it ever since, willing the dull pain to go away.

Michael kills the engine. I turn to him. God, I love this man. The feeling, which I had only just known this morning, blooms in my heart, as I stare at his frame.

He looks at me, concern heavy in his eyes. "Are you sure you're going to be okay? I don't want to leave you all alone here tonight."

He had been great today. From the call to now, he had been amazing. I lean in towards him and kiss him. I pour all my love and gratitude into it.

I lean back. "I'll be fine. I need this time alone. To get through this," lifting my sister's bag.

The paramedic had given it to me at the hospital.

Michael nods reluctantly. I touch Julia's car seat before opening the car door and getting out.

EMMA LENA

I enter my house and drop everything- my keys, my phone, my bag- on the kitchen counter. I walk to the living room and sit on the floor, my sister's bag in my lap. I take a deep breath in, as I open it. I see a host of different things, normal things like keys, lip gloss, a pack of gum.... a diary.

I pick up the diary and feel a tightening in my chest as I open it. Seeing my sister's handwriting and I realize this is the closest I have been to my sister in two years.

Tears stream down my face as I start to read. And then halfway through the first page, my hands still in shock.

No.

Chapter 19

MICHAEL

Four months ago.

The day after the wedding.

Michael's dream.

I pace the room like a madman. I run a hand through my hair, and let it rest on my head a bit. I look up at the ceiling, the single thought that had been in my head since yesterday, flashing like a neon sign in my mind again; *Why?*

I can't seem to get past that one single question. *Why?* It's like if I can just get the answer to that one question, this impatient raging madness in me will stop. Just the answer to that one question.

Everything had been great. *Hadn't it?* I shake my head as I start to pace again. *No, no, it had.* It had. I know it had. There is no way I wouldn't have known if it hadn't, I can read Laura like a book. She would have said something or shown something. Anything.

So, *why?*

I run a hand through my hair again. When I had walked away from the altar yesterday, my parents had cleared the remainder of the guests. I hadn't even known about that, I hadn't even been concerned about it. They had come in later, worry in both their eyes- a little bit of censure mixed with the worry in my dad's- and told me. I know it must have hurt them to do it, almost as it would have hurt me, and I know I should have been the one to do it, but I just didn't care about that then.

I still don't. All I care about is finding Laura and Julia. I think of Julia, her wide black eyes, her tiny toes and fingers. As soon as she had been placed in my arms two weeks ago, I had fallen in love with her. I had just tumbled into love with her. And now, I don't even know where she is.

I check my phone again, but still no message. Levy had said he would call if he had anything. He had been searching with me since yesterday.

Just then, the bell rings. My whole body, which was already coiled tight with tension, tense. I jump and lunge for the door. I throw it open, almost surprised in a corner of my mind, that it didn't fly off its hinges.

My brows furrow as I do not, at first, see anybody standing on my doorstep. I look around, but still nothing. I take a step forward, and my foot hits something. I look down, and I get the shock of my life.

Julia, swaddled in a blanket, eyes open and staring wide, at me, in a basket. On my porch. Slowly, I bend down, till I'm looking into her eyes. My baby. Julia.

Even with my heart hammering like crazy, I put my hands in the basket, lifting Julia slowly. "Hey, baby", I whisper, smiling at her. I cradle her to my chest and look into the basket. I see a folded piece of paper. My brows furrow in confusion even as my heart pounds loudly because of what I suspect the folded piece of paper means.

I pick the basket up with my free hand and turn to walk back inside.

I don't notice the woman standing behind a mailbox, opposite my house, staring at me with unshed tears in her eyes, as I go in.

I enter my house and close the door. I look around, trying to find a safe place to put Julia down. Finally, I look down at the basket still in my hand. I look at Julia, "You're going to have to stay in here a little longer, until I get something more suitable for you, okay, baby?"

I place her gently into the basket, and lower myself down beside her, on the floor. I gently rock the basket, even as I open up the folded piece of paper with my other hand. My hand is shaky, my chest tightens with pressure. I know opening this paper, and reading its content will forever change my life. I just know it.

I look at Julia again, maybe for courage, maybe for support, maybe for both. I look back down at the paper.

Dear Michael

This is not how I wanted it all to go between us. I want you to know that right off bat. I wanted it to go well, hell, I wanted us to have our happy-ever-after. And that is not something I always thought of. Ever. But I did, with you. I wanted to make it work, but giving reasons now why I couldn't, would just be excuses, and I don't make excuses. You know me. So, I'm just going to say 'I'm sorry.'

I'm sorry. I mean that.

And because I know you, and I know you're asking yourself, even now, 'why?' I am going to answer that question, give you peace in that. If that's all I can do for you right now, I'll take it.

You're not the reason why. I want different things from what you want. I tried to make myself want what you want, I tried to convince myself I could, but at the end of it, I just couldn't. Not even for you, Michael. You want the family, the holidays, the vacations, the firsts, kindergarten, middle school, high school, college, all of it. I didn't, do not, want that. When I think of all that, I get claustrophobic. I've never been afraid of tight spaces, but I guess my walls are of a different kind. And this life you want us to build together, that's my wall.

You don't deserve this. Me, leaving you this way. You're a good guy, Michael. And I'm sure you'll be an excellent father. You already love Julia more than life itself, I saw it in the hospital room. And that makes me happy. She deserves that.

Even though it doesn't look like it, I do love you.

I am truly sorry.

Laura.

Present. Friday. 4:00 a.m.

A loud knock sounds in my head, waking me up from my nightmare. I wake up with a start. I look around my dark room, trying to figure out where the hell I am. My eyes adjust to the darkness a bit, and I switch on the bedside lamp. The light floods the room, illuminating the shadows a bit.

I run a hand over my face. Jesus. *What the hell?* Why would I dream of that horrible day? That damned letter.

I grit my teeth as I sit up more on my bed. When I had taken Olivia to the hospital yesterday, I hadn't been allowed to follow her into the ICU. Family only. As a doctor, I understand why we say that to people, but yesterday, I hated that policy.

It had been clear as day when Olivia came out from the ICU, that she was even more shattered than when she had gone in. On the ride home, she hadn't said anything. She had been in shock most of the way.

I don't even know the name of her sister.

I run a hand through my hair. I know why I had a dream about Laura. After reading the letter she had left behind in the basket with Julia, I had finally known. It had been right there in my face that Laura left me. And while, over the next two weeks after that day, I had been heartbroken, I had also been worried sick.

Her leaving meant I had no way of knowing how she was doing and if she was okay. I had been worried that one day, a stranger would knock on my door, tell me she was gone, and shatter me still.

Which is what happened to Olivia today. Except it was a call that shattered her.

I hear the knock again, and realize it hadn't been in my head. Someone was knocking on my door.

My heart beats fast for reasons I don't even know, I get up from my bed, and walk out to the living room. I walk towards the door and open it to reveal Olivia.

My heart starts beating even more wildly. I take a look at her tear-stained face, her grief-filled eyes as she looks up at me. She is still wearing the same clothes I left her in just a few hours ago.

My brows furrow in confusion. "Olivia, what-?"

She lifts a diary, cutting off my words.

I look at the book, confused. I look back at Olivia.

"It's her. My sister's name is Laura Jenkins. It's her. She's the Laura you fell in love with."

Olivia's words pound in my head. *No, no, no.* I shake my head. "No, no, her name is Laura Evans. Not Jenkins. Evans."

Olivia's eyes widen, and then they narrow. "She changed her name. Evans is our mother's maiden name. She wanted to cut herself off completely, she even changed her name." Olivia whispers all these to herself. But the blood is already starting to roar in my ear.

If this is true, then that means.... the mother of my child is dead.

Chapter 20

MICHAEL & OLIVIA

Two weeks, and a day, later. Saturday. 10:35 p.m.

OLIVIA

I look around the carnival, bright blinding lights swirl all around me and loud music pumps out through the speakers, into the night. People, dressed in party clothes, some modest, some barely modest, some not even trying to be modest, all mixed, dancing and having a good time.

I bop my head to the music and sip from my red plastic cup. I know what's in it this time. Piña colada. I smile wryly as I remember my first-ever party on Catalina Island. I blow out a breath. Whew. That had been one wild night.

I drink from my cup again, deliberately blocking all thoughts of that night from my mind.

I can't think about him. It's been two weeks now, and I think I have all my emotions, or at least, most of them, under control. But, still not thinking about him. Even with two weeks, he's still too much to think about.

I smile as Alicia dances towards me. She is wearing a glittery short gown that stops at her knees, and colorful Jamaican beads hang from her neck, bouncing as *she* bounces. Her hair is let down in curly waves around her face, and her face is covered in face paint in the shape of a castle on one cheek, and a beach on the other cheek.

"Nice", I say, pointing at both cheeks.

Alicia laughs and nods her head in rhythm to the music. "Yeah! My other dream place to live in other than this place? A freaking castle!"

I laugh too. Alicia is such a force. She doesn't look like a doctor tonight.

The smile on her face dims down a bit, she places a hand on my arm. "You sure you're okay though?" I smile.

Alicia had been a great friend to me ever since the news of my sister's death two weeks ago. She has been a rock I hadn't even counted on. I know she and Deaton divided themselves between me and Michael, seeing as Michael had gotten a shock of his own that night. I've been glad ever since then that I got Alicia.

"I'm okay. We buried her the day before. My mom came over here, we decided she would have loved to be buried here. She always loved the ocean, and we know she would have loved this place." I take a deep breath. "I'm reading more of her diary these days, and I feel closer to her every day. I'm healing. Thank you for being there for me," looking into Alicia's eyes.

She smiles at me. "Always", she says simply.

I hug her, closing my eyes. Tears don't come. I have cried my heart out for the past two weeks, and now, I'm just moving on from here. Glad for friends, for a new life.

I open my eyes, and I see him. Michael, with Julia's stroller. My heart constricts.

MICHAEL

"Hey man", I accept the half-hug from Deaton. He bends at his waist, looking down into Julia's stroller. Julia's eyes are closed, she is sleeping. I put a sound blocker over her ears, so the loud music wouldn't disturb her.

I hadn't planned to come to the party tonight. Julia had been sleeping, and I hadn't even wanted to leave the house, much less go to a party. But, I ended up coming out for three reasons. First, I was in charge of cups and ice. A minute and probably ridiculous responsibility in the face of the grand scheme of things, but still a responsibility anyway. Who knew you could fuck up cups and ice? I almost did.

After the life-shattering-and-changing news about Olivia's sister being the same woman I had fallen in love with a year ago, and who bore me my child, I had been disorganized. As expected. I had not been able to function on the simple daily tasks, much less taking care of cups and ice for a party.

Deaton had saved my ass there though.

Secondly, the reason why I am out tonight is Alicia and Deaton. They are the planners of this party, they are my friends, and Deaton had been a hell of a rock these past two weeks. In my book, they were reasons, and more, for me to show up here tonight.

I and Deaton had had a moment yesterday when I thanked him for just being there for me these past two weeks. It had been uncomfortable, and I am not having a re-run of it again. But, he knows how grateful I am for him.

And the third reason is Olivia. God, that part of my life was, still is, messed up. Before that damning call, I had been having one of the best mornings of my life.

Waking up beside a beautiful woman, hearing her say she had no regrets about us, and having her look at me with emotion shining in her beautiful eyes.

A person's life could change in an instant, and that had been the case for me after that call. It had been one hell after the other. And now, I can't even look at my daughter without seeing Olivia.

It was messed up, and that's saying the least.

I look around at the party, the colourful scenes, the loud music, partying people, and I remember my first party on Catalina Island.

I remember the punch bowl, I remember looking down at the head of the blonde beside me, and watching her eye the bowl of pink liquid on the table. I remember saying 'I don't think you want to drink that'. I remember her hazel eyes, looking up at me. Into me. I remember the punch I had felt in my stomach as I looked into her eyes.

I raise my head, and I feel that punch, stronger now, in my gut, and I look into those eyes again.

OLIVIA

He's walking towards me.

Why is he walking towards me?

I look around, hoping someone- I don't know who, but anyone- would come to my rescue.

He is still coming towards me.

I look around desperately, wildly, like a person in search of a life raft in the middle of the ocean.

He stops in front of me.

"Olivia", he says my name. I register his voice in a part of my mind, but my focus is on Deaton, or rather Julia's stroller, as he passes by me with her.

I see a peak of her, just a tiny peak of her baby cuteness, and my heart clutches. Her eyes are closed, and the pink ear mufflers around her head just add to her angelic look of her.

I bring my eyes back slowly to Michael as Deaton walks away with her.

Grief in my eyes, I look up at him. "Why? Why are you here? Why did you bring her here?"

He seems confused by my last question, his brows furrow. He grabs my arm and pulls me a few feet away from the party. The noise from the party dims a bit.

Michael looks down into my eyes, his green eyes clear in the night.

"I came here to talk to you, Olivia. We haven't talked for two weeks now. I understand that you needed space after everything. Hell, I did too. But we need to talk. We need to make things right, so we can move on with our lives."

I look up at him, incredulous.

"Make things right? Move on with our lives? How is that possible, Michael? Tell me how in the world that is ever possible." I pace away from him, running a hand through my hair. I whirl back to face him. "I can't even look at her in the face and not have my heart squeeze like a fist is tightening around it!" When Michael looks at me, confused, I burst out. "Julia! I can't even look *Julia* in the face without seeing my sister!"

123

Tears don't come. As I said, I have cried every tear I can cry. But my heart, God, my heart is tightening so painfully.

Michael looks at me, calm, his green eyes fixed on me as he walks towards me.

"That is never going to go away, Olivia. Look at me", he puts his hands on my arms and shakes me lightly. I look into his eyes. "Laura is her mother. She is a part of Julia's life as much as we are. But she is gone, Olivia. Laura is gone, and every day, I am going to carry the weight of the guilt of not doing enough to keep her with me. Maybe it's justified, maybe it's not, but I'm going to carry it with me." He pauses and then continues. "But we are what matters right now. Right here, as we stand here, we are what matters. Do you love me, Olivia?"

I close my eyes to his question. He shakes me a bit again. I open my eyes and look up into his.

"Will you ever love me the way you loved her? I don't want that, I don't, but I can't help but wonder, will you? One day, will you wake up and remember I'm not her and hate me? Or worse, feel obligated to me. We met just two months ago, Michael. Two months. You had more than one year with her. And a baby."

"The love I felt for Laura is so vastly different from what I feel for you right now. They are not even remotely the same. I gave my all to Laura. Even when she didn't give hers back, I gave it all to her. That's not healthy. It's not healthy, nor is it even love. I know that now. Meeting you, knowing you, loving you, I know that now. And Julia, I love her more than life itself. I love her with all my heart. And you, I laid it all out on the table for you. And you picked me. Do you think I didn't see all the fears in your eyes? All the insecurities, the doubts. I saw them all, cause they were also reflected in mine. But you chose me. And I chose you right back. We chose each other. So, my question is, do you love me, Olivia?"

I look up into his eyes, as they remain steady on mine. My heart pounds in my chest, and I'm sure he can hear it. Maybe it is I who can hear *his* heart pounding in *his* chest.

I can't believe I, Olivia Jenkins, a cynic, a woman afraid of committing to anything in her life, am about to commit, not once, but twice, to the same man. In less than a month.

I smile, looking deep into Michael's eyes. "I love you, Michael."

He smiles, and my heart soars at the expression in his eyes. "I love you, Olivia."

I would commit a hundred times over to this man.

I grab his face in my hands and pull his face down to mine. I close the distance between our lips and kiss him.

He kisses me back, and all is right with the world. My head swims with emotions, my heart pounds, and I feel his heart pound beneath my hands.

I pull him even closer, kissing him deeper. I want to borrow into him, lose myself in him. I think of the life I'm going to build with this man, the firsts, the vacations, the holidays, kindergartens, middle schools, high schools, colleges, everything, and all of it.

I feel a delicious thrill run through me as his lips continue to kiss mine.

Our life will start over right here on Catalina Island. I just know we are going to live here. Michael loves this place as much as I do. And with Julia, our perfect little family will begin. With Laura, always in our hearts.

The End

Made in the USA
Columbia, SC
15 October 2023

24498524R00079